She'd gotten him.

Gotten to him with her nails-on-chalkboard-grating cheerfulness and her over-the-top optimism. Because Cavanaugh seemed to care about everything and everyone, she'd somehow managed to get to him. To burrow her way under his skin and take up residence.

He didn't want to be gotten.

He wanted to continue just as he was, being a dedicated detective working the cases he was assigned. He didn't need a social life. Just work, just the feeling that somehow, some way he was making the slightest bit of difference by tilting the balance between good and evil to the plus side just a fraction.

That was all he needed.

But now, with this woman—his partner—buzzing around in his life like an annoying hummingbird that wouldn't fly away, he needed more.

Wanted more.

Wanted *her,* he realized with a shock.

Dear Reader,

It's spring, love is in the air...and what better way to celebrate than by taking a break with Silhouette Special Edition? We begin the month with *Treasured*, the conclusion to Sherryl Woods's MILLION DOLLAR DESTINIES series. Though his two brothers have been successfully paired off, Ben Carlton is convinced he's "destined" to go it alone. But the brooding, talented young man is about to meet his match in a beautiful gallery owner—courtesy of fate...plus a little help from his matchmaking aunt.

And Pamela Toth concludes the MERLYN COUNTY MIDWIVES series with *In the Enemy's Arms*, in which a detective trying to get to the bottom of a hospital black-market drug investigation finds himself in close contact with his old high school flame, now a beautiful M.D.—she's his prime suspect! And exciting new author Lynda Sandoval (look for her Special Edition novel *One Perfect Man*, coming in June) makes her debut and wraps up the LOGAN'S LEGACY Special Edition prequels, all in one book—*And Then There Were Three*. Next, Christine Flynn begins her new miniseries, THE KENDRICKS OF CAMELOT, with *The Housekeeper's Daughter*, in which a son of Camelot—Virginia, that is—finds himself inexplicably drawn to the one woman he can never have. Marie Ferrarella moves her popular CAVANAUGH JUSTICE series into Special Edition with *The Strong Silent Type*, in which a female detective finds her handsome male partner somewhat less than chatty. But her determination to get him to talk quickly morphs into a determination to...get him. And in Ellen Tanner Marsh's *For His Son's Sake*, a single father trying to connect with the son whose existence he just recently discovered finds in the free-spirited Kenzie Daniels a woman they could *both* love.

So enjoy! And come back next month for six heartwarming books from Silhouette Special Edition.

Happy reading!

Gail Chasan
Senior Editor

Please address questions and book requests to:
Silhouette Reader Service
U.S.: 3010 Walden Ave., P.O. Box 1325, Buffalo, NY 14269
Canadian: P.O. Box 609, Fort Erie, Ont. L2A 5X3

Marie Ferrarella

THE STRONG SILENT TYPE

Silhouette®

SPECIAL EDITION®

Published by Silhouette Books

America's Publisher of Contemporary Romance

To Jessi and Nik,
who grew up much too fast.

Love, Mom

SILHOUETTE BOOKS

ISBN 0-373-24613-7

THE STRONG SILENT TYPE

Copyright © 2004 by Marie Rydzynski-Ferrarella

Books by Marie Ferrarella in Miniseries

ChildFinders, Inc.
A Hero for All Seasons IM #932
A Forever Kind of Hero IM #943
Hero in the Nick of Time IM #956
Hero for Hire IM #1042
An Uncommon Hero Silhouette Books
A Hero in Her Eyes IM #1059
Heart of a Hero IM #1105

Baby's Choice
Caution: Baby Ahead SR #1007
Mother on the Wing SR #1026
Baby Times Two SR #1037

The Baby of the Month Club
Baby's First Christmas SE #997
Happy New Year—Baby! IM #686
The 7lb., 2oz. Valentine Yours Truly
Husband: Optional SD #988
Do You Take This Child? SR #1145
Detective Dad World's Most
  Eligible Bachelors
The Once and Future Father IM #1017
In the Family Way Silhouette Books
Baby Talk Silhouette Books
An Abundance of Babies SE #1422

Like Mother, Like Daughter
One Plus One Makes Marriage SR #1328
Never Too Late for Love SR #1351

The Bachelors of Blair Memorial
In Graywolf's Hands IM #1155
M.D. Most Wanted IM #1167
Mac's Bedside Manner SE #1492
Undercover M.D. IM #1191

Two Halves of a Whole
The Baby Came C.O.D. SR #1264
Desperately Seeking Twin Yours Truly

*The Reeds
Callaghan's Way IM #601
Serena McKee's Back in Town IM #808

Those Sinclairs
Holding Out for a Hero IM #496
Heroes Great and Small IM #501
Christmas Every Day IM #538
Caitlin's Guardian Angel IM #661

The Cutlers of the Shady Lady Ranch
(Yours Truly titles)
Fiona and the Sexy Stranger
Cowboys Are for Loving
Will and the Headstrong Female
The Law and Ginny Marlow
A Match for Morgan
A Triple Threat to Bachelorhood SR #1564

*McClellans & Marinos
Man Trouble SR #815
The Taming of the Teen SR #839
Babies on His Mind SR #920
The Baby beneath the Mistletoe SR #1408

*The Alaskans
Wife in the Mail SE #1217
Stand-In Mom SE #1294
Found: His Perfect Wife SE #1310
The M.D. Meets His Match SE #1401
Lily and the Lawman SE #1467
The Bride Wore Blue Jeans SE #1565

*The Pendletons
Baby in the Middle SE #892
Husband: Some Assembly Required SE #931

The Mom Squad
A Billionaire and a Baby SE #1528
A Bachelor and a Baby SD #1503
The Baby Mission IM #1220
Beauty and the Baby IM #1668

Cavanaugh Justice
Racing Against Time IM #1249
Crime and Passion IM #1256
Internal Affair Silhouette Books
Dangerous Games IM #1274
The Strong Silent Type SE #1613

*Unflashed series

MARIE FERRARELLA

This RITA® Award-winning author has written over one
hundred and twenty books for Silhouette, some under the
name Marie Nicole. Her romances are beloved by fans
worldwide.

MEET THE CAVANAUGHS...

CAVANAUGH
JUSTICE

Detective **Teri Cavanaugh** loves a good conversation, but she loves a challenge even more. Can she get her gruff partner, Jack Hawkins, to warm up to her? Or will this sexy and oh-so-serious man show her a thing or two about his philosophy of less talk and more action?

Retired police chief **Andrew Cavanaugh** loves his children and hides from them his secret quest to find his long-lost love. Fifteen years ago his wife disappeared, and Andrew won't give up hope that she'll come home....

Rose "Claire" Cavanaugh went out for a drive fifteen years ago and found herself with a new identity and no recollection of her past. Can a kindly, handsome man who claims to be her husband bring her back to the fold?

* * *

**Let's not forget other members
of the Cavanaugh brood:
Callie (*Racing Against Time*, IM#1249),
Clay (*Crime and Passion*, IM#1256),
Patrick (*Internal Affair*, Silhouette Books)
and Rayne (*Dangerous Games*, IM#1274).**

Chapter One

There was no recognition in the woman's eyes.

Try as he might to will it there, Andrew Cavanaugh didn't see even the slightest hint of acknowledgment that he and she had grown up together, that the teasing and name-calling of two shy adolescents had masked the growing attraction they shared for one another.

There was no indication on her face that she remembered they had gotten married straight out of high school and that soon afterward, while he struggled to make his way up through the ranks of the Aurora police force, they'd been blessed with children. Five in total.

No indication that she even knew who he was or

that he'd spent the past fifteen years of his life searching for her, praying that she'd somehow managed to
escape the watery grave that had claimed the vehicle
she'd been driving that day.

She was Rose, his Rose, he was sure of it, even
though the name tag on her uniform proclaimed her
name to be Claire. She didn't belong in this diner.
She belonged home.

With him.

With her family.

She was his Rose, even though her hair was a little
less blond now than he remembered. Her eyes were
still as blue and her shape as supple as the day he
first made her his wife.

He could feel his heart aching as the woman
walked by him again, then paused and retrace her
steps.

"What will it be, mister?" the woman called Claire
asked in Rose's voice.

He desperately wanted to answer, "You," then de-
mand to know how she could look at him and not
feel what he was feeling, not throw her arms around
him the way he wanted to throw them around her. All
his training as a policeman, as a detective and then
as the chief of Aurora's police force strained to hold
him in check. To keep his hands from grasping her
shoulders and shaking her until the clouds lifted from
her eyes.

"Just a cup of coffee," he told her.

He watched as "Claire" placed a cup and saucer before him.

She smiled, wrenching his heart further, and asked, "Cream?"

He took his coffee black—he always had. Why didn't she remember that?

Patient, damn it. You've got to be patient, Andrew silently insisted.

He watched her slender fingers spread out on the counter as she waited for his reply. And then he knew what he needed to do.

"Yes, please."

With a nod of her head, sending her soft dark blond hair bobbing, the waitress placed a small metal container filled with cream beside his full cup. Then, reaching into the freshly cleaned utensils, she plucked out a teaspoon and placed it next to the container.

Leaving him with his coffee and his memories, she went to wait on the family of five who had just taken the booth beside the entrance.

Andrew left forty minutes later, having nursed his coffee and his memories for as long as he could. The coffee was poor to fair, the memories almost too agonizingly sweet to bear. He'd remained because he couldn't tear himself away.

And because he kept praying he'd see the light of recognition in her eyes.

But he didn't. He was going to have to arrive at his goal by other, less quick means.

The spoon "Claire" had handled was carefully wrapped up in a paper napkin and tucked into his pocket.

At bottom, Andrew Cavanaugh was an emotional man and unashamed of it. But he'd spent too many years as a cop not to recognize the need for hard evidence.

He had her fingerprints.

Detective Teri Cavanaugh stole a glance at her partner's heroic-in-a-superhero-sort-of-way profile as they came out of a hairpin turn.

Nothing.

No change of expression, no comment that the car he was driving had all but taken the turn on two wheels and probably come close to turning over. Nothing. It was like being partnered with a sphinx. A very sexy, sensual-looking sphinx, but a sphinx nonetheless.

It had been nine months since they had first been teamed up by some ironic whimsy of fate and her uncle Brian Cavanaugh, the chief of detectives. Nine months and Detective First Class Jack Hawkins had uttered maybe three dozen sentences on his own without having had the words pried out of him with a crowbar.

She sighed and shook her head. You'd think that after spending her childhood in the never-ending company of four brothers and sisters and six cousins, she would have welcomed these quiet moments of respite with the Aurora Police Department's version of a mannequin.

But noise was her element—it always had been. She thrived on chaos and confusion, found herself thinking better that way. Detective Jack Hawkins, however, seemed to thrive on silence. The very same atmosphere that was guaranteed to drive her crazy.

Just as it was now.

Silence made her itchy, restless. She would have had trouble sitting still even if he wasn't racing to a call dispatch had just taken.

Enough, she thought, completely abandoning her plan not to be the first to talk today but to wait him out. There weren't enough minutes in the year for that.

"Do you realize that you haven't said ten words since you came on duty this morning?"

Hawk spared her a glance only after enough beats had gone by to convince Teri that he was going deaf and hadn't heard her.

"Don't see the need. You're doing fine on your own," he answered without even a hint of a smile on his lips.

Annoyance had her shifting again, just before they flew through a yellow light. She blew out a breath. "Damn it, Hawk, I don't like carrying on monologues. A little input once in a while would be nice."

His wide, muscular shoulders rose and fell in less than the blink of an eye. "Yeah, well, we can't always have what we want."

She frowned. Lately, she thought, she'd done a lot of frowning. And this statue of a partner had a lot to do with that. "You stand a better chance of getting whatever it is you want if you vocalize it."

Hawk allowed himself one swift glance in her direction before he looked back on the road. What he wanted was for her to stop prodding at him, to accept things the way they were and to maybe shut up for a while, while he still had his sanity. The woman talked more than any three other people he knew. It didn't help his mood any that lately she seemed to be getting under his skin more and more. Not just because of how much she talked, but just by being. There was an itch growing within him, an itch he didn't much care for and one he knew he couldn't scratch. Ever.

His voice was stony, completely devoid of emotion. "Not from where I'm looking."

And just where is that? she was tempted to ask, not that she figured he would get her an answer. Hawk didn't do well when it came to give and take. Everything she knew about Jack Hawkins she'd gotten by hacking into his personnel file.

Okay, she had to admit that the man hadn't had an easy time of it. Orphaned at a young age when a drug dealer killed both of his parents, Hawk had swiftly been incorporated into the system when no relatives came to claim him. In effect he'd been given a one-way ticket into hell, to survive as best he could.

That he'd gone on to become a police detective rather than a drug pusher himself was a credit to the man, and she would have been the first to praise him. However, as far as she could tell, he hadn't made the full transition from the dark side to the light even after he'd reached this plateau. And after nine months in his company, she was still utterly committed to the quest of dragging the black-haired, icy-blue-eyed man into that light. Or die trying.

It was on days like today that she was fairly certain it was going to wind up being the latter.

Teri saw another corner coming and she braced herself. "Then maybe you need to take another look, a clearer one this time."

"Let's just concentrate on the home invasion in progress," Hawk advised without the benefit of giving her another glance.

Teri held on as her partner took the next corner sharply. The man might behave like a monk who was determined to observe a vow of silence at all costs, but he certainly didn't drive like one. She braced both hands against the dashboard as he took another quick right.

He all but stole her breath away. The thought evoked an unconscious smile. There were days he did that when he wasn't driving at all. But that was something she couldn't allow to surface. It would throw the partnership right out the window.

They were on their way to a home invasion that was still in progress, having been alerted to it thanks to a call made by one of the victims, a brave little ten-year-old girl who, as far as Teri was concerned, had more on the ball than most adults.

It was the fifth such home invasion in Aurora in less than a month. This time, the robbery was taking place in an upscale apartment complex on the west side. Dispatch had the little girl, who was hiding with her cordless telephone receiver in a closet, on the line, allowing them to get a heads-up on what was happening as it took place.

Dispatch had just narrowed down the perimeter and confirmed the address less than two minutes ago. It was enough to make Hawk press down on the accelerator the rest of the way.

As cars frantically scrambled out of the path of the oncoming vehicle and its siren, Teri tried not to wonder if they were going to arrive in one piece.

"Think it's the same ones who pulled the past four jobs?" she asked, slamming her hands back on the dashboard as Hawk made a razor-sharp left.

Horns blared at them from all directions, the sound blending in with the screeching of brakes.

He didn't even appear to think about the question. For once, his answer was fired out. "Probably."

Most people knew enough to quit while they were ahead, but those on the other side of the law were a special breed. The brains they were issued at birth weren't the garden variety that enabled them to exercise restraint, to consider consequences instead of gains.

She shook her head as she saw scenery whiz by.

Not a single red light had caught them. "I guess success makes you bold."

Hawk was tempted to ask just what it was that had made *her* so bold and brassy, but he knew he'd probably get an answer several paragraphs longer than he was willing to bargain for. So he kept the question to himself, letting it die a natural death.

He wondered if she knew that he'd be willing to talk more if she talked less. Maybe it was just as well things went on this way. Talking led to places he wasn't willing to go.

For the life of him, Hawk had no idea what the chief had been thinking, teaming them up like this. The man was her uncle, for God's sake, he had to have a clue as to what she was like. For his part, Hawk came home every night, thinking about headache tablets and missing his old partner, a man who knew the value of silence and didn't speak until he was spoken to. In three years he and Edmunds hadn't exchanged as many words as were wont to fly out of Cavanaugh's mouth in three hours.

He damned Edmunds for getting in harm's way and then deciding the gunshot wound had been an omen that he'd used up his share of luck. Edmunds was now behind a desk, pushing a pen, which he found preferable to pushing up daisies, he said. The request for a desk job coincided with Cavanaugh's partner retiring. From what he'd heard, it was her second retiree. Hell, he would have retired, too, if it meant finally getting a little peace and quiet—and putting a lid on this damn restlessness he felt inside.

Reaching his destination, Hawk abruptly brought the unmarked squad car to a halt in front of the building in question. They had beaten the uniforms getting here, but then he'd expected nothing less. That had been his intent all along.

The Wongs' apartment, according to the terrified daughter who placed the call, was located on the second floor—2E. Hawk lost no time, jumping out of the vehicle and slamming the door in his wake. He didn't bother to look over his shoulder to see if the blond, blue-eyed bane of his existence was behind him. There was no need. If he'd learned nothing else in the past nine months, it was that the woman stuck like glue.

Probably had something to do with the fact that the rest of her family was in law enforcement, he reasoned. She'd been raised teething on a night stick and obviously felt she had something to prove.

Well, not to him. The one thing he would have liked her to prove was that she had the brains most people were born with. That meant not rushing into the heart of danger every time it reared its ugly head.

That he did was another matter. After all, he was a man. Men were supposed to do this kind of thing. Besides, he hadn't anything to lose. The way she talked, Cavanaugh loved life. That meant she had everything to lose.

He, on the other hand, had never loved life. He

tolerated it, just as it tolerated him. As far as he was concerned, he and life were nothing more than less than friendly adversaries.

Ignoring the startled inquiry of the doorman, Hawk tore into the building and quickly took the stairs to the second floor. The echo of footsteps told him she was right behind him.

His eyes took in everything in one swift, sweeping glance. The stately hallway before apartment 2E looked ready for photographing. Peaceful, elegant, it seemed an unlikely setting for a home invasion. Which was just what made it ripe for one.

Motioning Teri to the left side of the wide door while he took the right, Hawk strained to hear the sounds of discord coming from inside the apartment. Just the faintest of whimpers seeped into the air. His eyes met Teri's. She nodded, indicating that she'd heard it, as well.

Holding his fingers up, Hawk did a silent count to three, then spun and kicked open the door, his service revolver poised to fire at anything that moved. He yelled out, "Police!"

His voice swiftly drowned in the onslaught of screams, curses and confusion.

In a split second, Teri saw six people, two elderly, two middle-aged and two children, in various stages of terror, frozen in place. Their arms were raised above their heads and they were obviously the victims rather than perpetrators.

Two others were fleeing to the end of the apartment—toward the apartment's fire escape, if she didn't miss her guess.

"Freeze!" Hawk shouted, but neither of the two men did.

Instead, both men, small, agile and athletic, propelled themselves through the open window and were gone in less time than it took for the scene to register.

Hawk was in hot pursuit. "Stay here," he tossed over his shoulder, expecting her to obey. He should have known better.

"And when the hell did you become the boss of me?" Teri asked. Half a step behind, she followed him up the fire escape to the roof where the robbers had gone less than a minute before.

Hawk didn't bother answering her, knowing it was useless to waste the energy or the air. Instead, he was focused on the two burglars who moved with the speed of men who had done this kind of thing more than once before. He was convinced that these were the men who had been reported breaking into homes, terrorizing their marks before they made their escape.

Grasping the black, newly repainted railing, he swiftly made his way up.

Sick, sick people, he thought, having less regard for the men he was chasing than he would for a beetle that crossed his path.

If he could have gotten a clear shot, he would have tried to wound the one closest to him in the leg. But if he took the time to aim, they would get too far ahead of him and he wasn't about to risk firing wildly.

What went up came down if it didn't find a target and there were innocent bystanders on the street watching this minidrama unfold.

Why didn't they all go home and just let him do his job?

Reaching the roof, Teri scanned it from one end to the other, her heart pounding wildly in her chest. The area appeared almost eerily still. She'd expected to see the two robbers trying to make the daring leap from one roof to the other. Buildings in this part of the city were structured close together enough for the reckless to attempt a leap.

Nothing came but the sounds from the street below.

That and a pigeon circling around overhead, looking for somewhere to land.

And then suddenly, Teri saw the glint of sunlight hitting metal. It was coming from behind the raised skylight.

Her heart froze. They were going to shoot him. Instinct rather than cold observation kicked in and she shoved Hawk out of the way.

"Gun!" she yelled by way of a warning and an explanation as Hawk went down, uttering a very terse oath centered around her.

The second she got the word out, a volley of gunfire echoed in its wake.

Out in the open, exposed, Hawk quickly darted toward the roof's entrance.

Teri fell in behind him, although not as quickly as he would have figured she would have. Ordinarily, the woman was like his unshakable shadow, always less than half a breath behind, more than likely usually half a breath ahead. Concern instantly reared its head. Why was she dragging like that?

Sending a hail of bullets in the direction of the skylight, attempting to keep the burglars pinned down, Hawk looked behind him toward Teri. Like as not, he figured she probably saved him from getting shot. He owed her and he always paid up what he owed.

"Thanks," he mumbled.

For a moment, she didn't hear him. The gunfire and pain blotted almost everything else out. And there was this strange buzzing in her ears that came accompanied by volleys of heat. When his words finally managed to echo in her brain, she forced a smile to her lips.

"Too much paperwork involved when your partner dies on you."

Cavanaugh's voice was strained. Even over the gunfire he could hear it. Hawk looked at her again, more closely this time.

And saw the blood that stained her jacket.

A barrage of curses materialized in his head, masking the deep concern he felt. "Damn it, are you hurt?"

She forced a smile to her lips. Was that concern? Sure it was. Looked bad on your record, two partners getting shot in less than a year.

"Just ketchup," she managed to quip. "I'm a sloppy eater."

Damn it, she was cracking jokes when that scum had just shot her. Shot her with a bullet that had been meant for him. She could have been killed.

Incensed, Hawk swung back around and began discharging his weapon in rapid succession, keeping the two home invaders trapped behind the skylight as he rushed them.

Clutching her weapon with both hands, Teri followed him in his charge, summoning adrenaline and exercising mind over matter. She told herself over and over again that her side didn't feel as if it were on fire.

But it did. This wound hurt every bit as badly as when Clay, her twin brother, sent her flying from their tree house. They'd been ten at the time, embroiled in a heated argument she no longer recalled. All she remembered from the incident was that she broke her arm and her father had been furious with Clay. That had helped alleviate the pain somewhat.

No, she amended silently, gritting her teeth together, this definitely hurt more.

Firing as rapidly as she could, holding her side now as she went, Teri did her best to match Hawk step for step. She managed to keep the burglars pinned down as he gained ground.

"Damn it, woman, get back!" He roared the order, knowing in his heart she wouldn't listen. Cavanaugh never listened. Wasn't it enough that she'd gotten shot? Did she want to get killed, too? Fear echoed in his brain.

The next moment, he got the drop on both burglars, ordering them to drop their weapons or suffer the consequences.

One threw down his weapon, raising his hands above his head. "Don't shoot, don't shoot," he begged them each in turn.

The second man held on to his weapon, his dark eyes darting from one police detective to the other.

Hawk thought of Teri and what could have been. "C'mon," he growled, pinning the second man down with a glare from his icy-blue eyes as much as with his gun. "Give me an excuse. Just one excuse."

Clearly shaken, the second man threw down his weapon and raised his hands. His eyes never left Hawk's. "Okay, I did like you said. Just don't shoot me."

"Step away from the guns," Teri ordered, waving them back with her own weapon. Only when the men complied did she allow herself to look in Hawk's direction. She did her best to brazen it out. "Good imitation of Dirty Harry. My father would really like you."

Picking up the burglars' weapons, Hawk didn't trust himself to answer immediately.

Chapter Two

It seemed as if only seconds had gone by. Suddenly, the roof was alive with uniformed personnel that poured out from both the fire escape and the rooftop entrance.

The extra commotion only added to the lightheaded feeling Teri vainly struggled to keep at bay.

She was careful to keep her eyes trained forward. Any quick movements on her part seemed guaranteed to make her lose her bearings and fall.

"About time you got here," she said to one of the policeman. "The fun's all over."

The officer closest to her took one look at the growing red splotch to the right of her rib cage. "Looks like it just started. In case you missed it, you've been shot.'' Concerned, he raised his eyes to her face. ''You better get yourself to a hospital.''

Drawing in a deep breath was out of the question. Breathing itself was becoming a challenge for her. She was deathly afraid she was going to pass out.

''Yeah, I guess I'd better.'' She couldn't manage the sentence without a sense of dread descending over her. The hospital was the last place she wanted to go.

''Finally, something sensible,'' Hawk said.

Pressing her hand over her wound to stop the ooze of blood, Teri slowly turned to look at her partner. She wasn't about to give in to this pain; she wasn't. ''Wow, you volunteered something on your own.''

''And you're being smart. Red letter day for both of us.'' Hawk stepped back as a patrolman snapped handcuffs on the two suspects. As he did, he glanced at Teri's face. The last time he'd gone to the mountains, the snow hadn't looked as white as her skin. Fear put in another appearance, stronger this time. ''Hey, Cavanaugh, are you all right?''

Her knees suddenly went soft on her and someone had tilted the sky, leaving it at almost a right angle. Afraid of falling and embarrassing herself, Teri grabbed on to the first thing she came in contact with.

It turned out to be Hawk.

''Yeah.'' She exhaled the word shakily. ''Just peachy.'' She needed a few minutes, just a few minutes to get a grip, then she would be all right. Pressing her other hand harder against her wound, she managed a tight smile. "Who turned the roof on? It's spinning."

The same police officer looked at Hawk uncertainly. "Want me to call the paramedics?" Hawk's glare ended any debate that might have emerged on the pros and cons of the situation. "I'll call the paramedics," the officer volunteered.

She didn't want a fuss, and least of all, she didn't want to be excluded from the action. "I don't need paramedics, just a bullet to bite on."

"You need to dig it out of your side first." With the suspects safely handcuffed, one of the officers raised a quizzical brow in Hawk's direction. Frowning, Hawk waved the patrolmen on their way. "Take them to the precinct and book 'em."

There were statements to take from the victims in 2E and that was best done while the memory of events and the order they transpired in was still fresh. But Teri had been shot, and who knew how bad it really was? He had to see to it that she was taken care of. He wasn't about to leave her here and expect her to get herself to the ground floor. Right now, she didn't look capable of getting herself two feet from where she was standing. Or sinking.

Turning toward Teri, he took hold of her by the arm. "I'll take you downstairs."

"I can walk," she retorted, but two steps toward the rooftop entrance proved her to be a liar. She grabbed Hawk's arm again. "Okay, maybe not."

He didn't have time for this—to help her take tiny

steps to the roof's stairwell and down the flight to the elevator—and she was obviously in no shape to do it on her own.

With an annoyed, unintelligible grunt, Hawk never hesitated. He swept her up into his arms. She didn't weigh much, but then, he hadn't expected that she would. She was five foot three something and filled with hot air. Hot air was never very heavy.

Teri wanted to protest, but she couldn't find the energy. This was a whole lot better than trying to concentrate on placing one foot in front of the other. "I had no idea you were this gallant."

He ignored the looks of officers who were vacating the roof. He'd never much cared about what people thought one way or another, as long as they didn't get in his way. "I'm not. I'm pragmatic."

She smiled at him. He could say what he wanted, but she knew he cared about her. This was a whole other side of Hawk she'd never seen before. Too bad it had taken her getting shot for it to emerge. Something warm began to stir within her. "Was that one of King Arthur's Knights of the Round Table?"

She was babbling more than usual. "Are you getting delirious on me?"

"Delirious," she repeated as if trying to remember. "First handmaiden to Queen Guinevere, right?"

Either she really was delirious, or she was taking this opportunity to yank his chain. Either way, it didn't improve his mood. "Shut up before I think better of this and throw you off the roof."

"I'm shutting."

Trying very hard to ignore the fire that was eating up her side, Teri threaded her arms around his neck. She was fairly certain that the bullet had only grazed her, but that didn't change the fact that everything was spinning around her. Even though she would have hated to admit it, she wasn't that much of a trouper when it came to looking at her own spilled blood. She liked keeping it just where it belonged. In her veins.

She forced a smile to her lips as she looked at him. "Am I supposed to be out of my head right now so I can't remind you of this gallantry later on?"

Coming to the door, he let one of the remaining policemen open it for him. He ignored the look the man gave him. Ignored, too, the strange feeling he felt in response to holding her against him like this. "Far as I'm concerned, you're *always* out of your head, Cavanaugh."

Maybe if she talked, she could keep her head from spinning off. "Spoken like a true gentleman. At least you're making progress." He was taking the stairs down and each step vibrated along her side. "That was almost a complete sentence. There's hope for you yet, Hawk." She sucked in her breath as he jostled her.

She was hurting, he thought, frustrated because he was powerless to help her. He didn't like seeing her in pain like this. "Hang in there," he muttered.

"Don't have much choice, do I?" Her mind

jumped from topic to topic like a frog going from one lily pad to another in a pond. She thought of word leaking back about her wound. It would spread in no time like a prairie fire across dry grass. "Oh, God, Dad's going to freak."

The moment she said it, a protectiveness gripped her heart. Andrew Cavanaugh had had enough to contend with in his lifetime. She didn't want this added to the pile, at least not until he could see for himself that she was all right. Since she lived at home, there was no way she could hide this indefinitely, but she wanted to spare him as much as possible for as long as possible.

She looked at Hawk, her eyes imploring him. "Don't call my father and tell him about this."

They'd finally made it to the landing. He'd gone as slowly as he dared. Hawk brought her over to the elevator. Angling for the best position in order to get at the button, he raised Teri up slightly in his arms, then pressed. He'd bench-pressed twice her weight just yesterday. Didn't she eat?

"I have no intentions of calling your father."

No, he wouldn't, she realized. He wouldn't see the need for it. Hawk didn't understand the kind of closeness a family like theirs generated. She wondered if he'd ever experienced anything remotely resembling closeness amid all the foster families he'd been shipped off to during his youth.

Probably not.

She felt something stir in her heart. It wasn't pity,

just an overwhelming amount of sympathy, but he probably wouldn't have understood that, either. In an odd way, he appeared to be content in his life with things just the way they were.

But she wasn't.

"Sorry, I forgot who I was talking to," she mumbled. Teri withdrew her arms from his neck, but he made no move to set her on the floor. Given a choice, she would have rather remained this way, in his arms, for a host of reasons. But it ate at her independence. "You can put me down now," she said softly.

His eyes met hers and she almost expected him to try to argue her out of it. He didn't. Instead, without a word, he allowed her to test her own legs.

And find herself wanting. Teri's knees all but buckled out from under her.

"Any other bright ideas?" he asked as he picked her up into his arms again.

"Several, but they all involve less clothing." She gave him a sexy, sidelong glance to mask the pain she felt shooting up and down her entire left side. It was a joke, purely a joke, or so she told herself. But for one moment, something telegraphed itself between them, something almost erotic. The next moment, it was gone and he was looking at her with what appeared to be confusion. "Gotcha," she muttered in triumph.

He made no comment. With Teri, it was safer that way. He glared instead at the light, which testified that the elevator car had not left the second floor in all this time. More than likely, it'd temporarily been commandeered by the officers going over the victims' apartment. There was no telling when they would release the elevator. Probably not before checking out the rest of the building in case the burglars had accomplices who had fled to other floors.

He also didn't know how long he would be required to remain standing here with Teri. And she was in no shape to wait indefinitely. Making up his mind, Hawk headed back toward the stairwell. When he reached it, he pushed open the door with his back.

Teri stared at him. "Where are we going?"

"To never-never land," he said between clenched teeth. There she went, asking more questions, butting heads with him at every turn. Why couldn't she just be cooperative and pass out like any normal person in her place would have?

Teri blinked. "A joke. You made a joke. I must be dying. Is it that serious?"

Hawk sighed, trying hard not to jostle her any more than he had to. He didn't even look at his partner. "If I said yes, would you shut up?"

She wanted to thread her arms back around his neck to secure herself, but she felt that if she didn't keep pressing her hand against her side, everything would come tumbling out. "Now you're starting to hurt my feelings, Hawk. And just when we were getting so close, too."

"We're not getting close," he informed her tersely, taking the next set of stairs down. "I don't get close."

And because there was a real danger of that happening here, he put out a special effort to keep her at arm's length.

Deep down, he didn't really believe that, she thought. It was just something he'd talked himself into. "Even the Lone Ranger had Tonto."

This time he did look at her. "I'm not interested in having anyone."

She thought of the way the women at the precinct looked at him when he wasn't paying attention. Which was all of the time.

"Oh, well, that's a shame, because there are plenty of people interested in having you." Determined not to let him know how much this was hurting, she pushed harder against the wound praying it would stop radiating pain.

He almost slipped and told her she was delirious again, but stopped himself in time. "You don't know what you're talking about."

She gave him that smile, that knowing, almost smug smile that said she was privy to some kind of inside information that he wasn't. The one that never failed to test the parameters of his temper and find him seriously lacking. The one that got under his skin no matter how much he tried to keep it out.

"You know," she said in an almost breathless manner that concerned him the moment he heard it, "for a police detective, you're not very observant. Female people," she finally elaborated. "You don't seem to notice all the heads that turn whenever you come into the room, partner. You definitely raise blood pressures.''

He gave her a look that would have silenced a babbling brook, but had no effect on her. ''You're raising mine right now.''

She chose to interpret his comment the way she knew would drive him crazy. ''What a lovely thing to say, Hawk.''

''It wasn't meant to be.''

Why did five flights feel so endless? She was surprisingly light, even in boots and a winter jacket, but he was being careful not to jostle her any further, and that took time and effort. He wasn't happy about having to hold her against him like this. He had her so close, the blood from her wound had gotten onto his clothing.

It wasn't the blood he was concerned about. With a little cold water, a lot of soaking, blood washed out. It was breathing in that cologne of hers—the one she swore she didn't wear—that was getting to him. It made the closed-in area of the stairwell almost suffocating for him. He responded to her in ways he didn't want to even think about.

In ways he didn't want to respond. He couldn't think of her as a woman, he reminded himself.

He couldn't not.

Teri took a deep breath. The dizziness was beginning to pass slightly. Maybe she was getting her second wind, she reasoned. She looked at Hawk. ''Let me walk down the rest of the way,'' she said. ''I don't want you naming your hernia after me.''

This wasn't even up for discussion. If he let her try to stand up, he was fairly certain she was going to go down like a stone. He would have bet his next month's pay on it.

''You weigh twelve and a half pounds—don't worry about it.''

She wasn't exactly worried, but this definitely had the makings of something he was going to use to his advantage throughout their partnership. ''This isn't something you're going to let me live down.''

She was out of her head, wasn't she? he thought. Other partners had rapports where there was a certain amount of give and take, of banter. He would have liked nothing better than to spend his time with her in completely silence except for the dispatch radio.

''This isn't something I ever intend to talk about. Ever,'' he underscored.

She tried to guess at his reason. ''Don't like people reminding you that you're kind?''

''Don't like people being pains in the butt,'' he countered.

Jack Hawkins was a hard nut to crack, she thought. But here he was, being nice to her. He could have waited for the elevator, could have waited for the paramedics to arrive on the roof, for that matter, instead of taking it upon himself to carry her down five flights of stairs to the ground floor. Six if they counted the set of stairs that had led from the roof to the fifth floor. Which meant the big lug cared.

"You can huff and puff all you want, Hawk, but I've got your number. You're not the big bad wolf you pretend to be."

Reaching the final landing, he paused long enough to look her right in the eye. She had to get over this noble image of him she was trying to paint. It got in his way.

"I don't waste my time pretending." So saying, he pushed down on the door handle with his elbow, opening the door that led out into the lobby.

Hawk could protest all he wanted; she knew better. But she played along, her mouth curving. "What you see is what you get, huh?"

He didn't bother looking at her. Instead, he walked by the doorman, whose mouth dropped open when he saw the wounded woman in Hawk's arms. "Right."

"Wrong," she countered just as the ambulance came into view.

Seeing journey's end, Hawk almost sighed with relief. Not long now.

The doors of the stark-white vehicle with its red letters popped open. One of the two paramedics assigned to it jumped out.

Hawk deposited her inside the rear of the ambulance.

"She's all yours," he announced, backing away with his arms slightly raised, like a rodeo star who had just tied up a calf. "Best of luck to you."

A ray of panic flashed between the shafts of pain vying for possession of her. He was leaving.

"You're not coming?"

If he didn't know any better, he would have said she looked scared. But if he'd learned nothing else these very long nine months, he'd learned that Theresa Cavanaugh did not get scared. Or, and this was probably more likely, if she did, she never showed it.

"Someone has to fill in the reports."

Hawk began to walk away when he saw her wince as the paramedic slid off her coat. There was blood everywhere, spearing on his guilt. If it hadn't been for her pushing him out of the way, he would have been the one with the wound. And, more than likely, his would have been more serious. He was taller than she was. It didn't take much of a stretch of the imagination to realize that the bullet would have probably found its way into his gut.

The encroaching panic continued spinning out its web, swirling around her. She saw the way Hawk looked at her wound and guessed at what he was thinking, if not saying. She shamelessly used it to her advantage. "We caught the bad guys, Hawk. The paperwork can wait for a couple of hours."

The paramedic was administering to her wound, bandaging it up as quickly as possible. Hawk averted his eyes from the exposed area, giving her her privacy. "Why do you want me to come with you?"

She could lie. She could make a joke about it. But right now, she needed to have him come with her. To chase the specters away. So she went with the truth and hoped it would work.

"I need someone to hold my hand," she told him honestly. "I never liked hospitals. People die in hospitals."

He wasn't sure if she was putting him on again or not. But there was a look in her eyes that didn't allow him to retreat the way he wanted to. He couldn't just abandon her.

Hawk looked around the area. The so-called suspects had been placed in the back of a squad car that was about to pull out. There was protocol to follow, he reminded himself.

The paramedic was urging her onto the gurney. "Only the good die young," Hawk informed her. "I'll catch up with you."

To his surprise, she said nothing. She only continued looking at him. Continued looking even as the paramedic closed the doors, severing eye contact.

"Ah, hell," Hawk bit off, shaking his head. Spinning around on his heel, he looked around until he saw a face he recognized. Quickly, he crossed to the heavyset detective. "Hey, Mulrooney, tell Mr. and Mrs. Wong that I'll be back to take their statements after they've had a chance to pull themselves together."

Mulrooney looked surprised that Hawk wasn't on his way back upstairs. "Where are you going?"

Hawk clenched his teeth together. He didn't like

having to explain himself, especially when he was having trouble understanding is own motivation.

"My partner's been shot. I'm heading out to the hospital to make sure she's all right."

Again Mulrooney nodded, this time looking at the ambulance that had just peeled away, its siren going full blast. He grinned broadly. Everyone liked Teri Cavanaugh. The same couldn't be said about her partner. "Trade assignments with you, Hawkins."

Hawk made no answer. Given his choice, he would have liked to take Mulrooney up on that. The latter had the better end of the deal.

Muttering a few choice things under his breath, Hawk hurried to his car.

Her side throbbed wildly to the beat of the *1812 Overture* by the time the ambulance pulled into the parking lot behind Aurora Memorial Hospital's ER. Even so, Teri braced herself as the paramedic went to open the rear doors.

This was the hospital where they had brought her uncle Mike the day he'd been shot.

This was the hospital Uncle Mike had died in.

The shooting had happened less than a month after her mother's car had crashed through the guardrail and gone over the side, to be submerged in the river. Teri had been twelve at the time and the two events combined had overwhelmed her almost completely. She'd come away with a lasting phobia of hospitals.

That same phobia was alive and well now, fifteen

years later, even though she knew that logic dictated that she come here to be treated.

Logic was one thing, but superstitious and phobias didn't understand logic.

"You better lie down." The paramedic who'd treated her placed a hand on her shoulder, intending to help her get comfortable.

She stiffened as if she'd been shot again. There was no way in hell they were going to strap her down to the gurney, not while she was conscious.

"I can get out on my own power."

She didn't want to be held down while they wheeled her in, not as long as she could walk. There was something helpless about being pushed in through the electronic doors, not being able to move a muscle.

She pressed her lips together, her body tense, her side stinging like crazy as the rear doors opened, braced for the inevitable wave of fear to hit her with the force of a tidal wave.

What she wasn't prepared for was to see Hawk standing there when the doors opened.

Chapter Three

He came.

The words vibrated in her brain, bringing with them a wave of relief and happiness. Teri waved away the paramedic who'd just tried to get her to lie on the gurney.

"I'll sit, but I won't lie down." She looked at Hawk who stepped back as the gurney was brought out of the ambulance. The dread drained out of her. She didn't have to face going in alone. "Did you forget something?"

"Yeah, my better judgment." He'd seen the relief that had leaped into her eyes, so intense that for a second it stopped him in his tracks. What was that about? Was she actually afraid of hospitals? He hadn't thought she was afraid of anything. It was part of the woman's appeal.

The paramedics were pushing her through the doors. And Hawk was not fading back into the parking lot—he was coming in with her. "What about the statements?" she asked.

"I told Mulrooney to tell the victims I would be by later to take them."

There were nurses and attendants scattered throughout the rear of the ER. Hawk flashed his badge at the one closest to them. The tall woman in dark green livery immediately pointed the paramedics to an open bed.

"We," Teri corrected him. "We would be by later."

There was brave, and then there was stupid. Cavanaugh had crossed the line. "Thinking of going somewhere, Superwoman?" Before she could answer, he asked, "Don't you think that you've done enough damage to yourself for one day?"

Again she waved back hands that reached out to help. "I can do this," she told the nurse who eyed her dubiously. Bracing herself against the mattress, she slid off the gurney and onto the hospital bed. Her body hated her for it. "It's not like I stood there, daring the guy to shoot me. Hawk. I took a bullet for you."

Guilt corkscrewed into him a little further. "Yeah, you did."

Sitting on the bed, she read the look in his eyes. "And you feel guilty, don't you?"

"Guilt's not in my file folder." He wasn't about to have her poking around in his head, thinking she could read him. There were things there she couldn't see.

Teri laughed shortly. "Don't tell me that. I've seen it often enough on the faces of my brothers to know guilt when I see it." Pain dragged spiked shoes across her side. Teri waited to catch her breath. It wasn't easy. "No need for guilt. You would have done the same for me." And then she surprised him by taking hold of his hand in hers. "Thanks."

The simple gratitude he both saw in her eyes and heard in her voice stirred something within him and made him uneasy. He shrugged her words away.

Emotions of any kind, other than cold, steely anger, made him uncomfortable. They always had. He'd never had any outlet for them. The parents he'd once wanted so desperately to notice him, to get themselves clean and turn him and them into a real family, had rejected him. They had ignored him for as far back as he could remember. Instead, they had more interest in the drugs that could remove them from their world and take them to somewhere he had no desire to go.

Even as a kid, he'd known that drugs were bad. He'd watched firsthand as first his father, then his mother became firmly entrenched—because of drugs—in the land of the living dead.

He'd attempted, in his own way, to make his parents come around. He'd cooked, cleaned and tried to take care of them. There were tiny glimmers, moments when he thought things were finally on the right path, but in the end, all his efforts came to nothing.

When he was just twelve, a drug dealer, enraged because his parents were into him for several hundred dollars, had killed them both. Snuffed out their lives without so much as a peep from either for them. They were that far gone into their make-believe worlds.

And he had seen it all through the crack created by the doorjamb and a closet door.

He'd tried to wake them, knowing even as he desperately shook his mother, then his father, that they were both dead. And he'd been the one who had called 911 to report their murders.

Any shred of childhood he might have still possessed died with his parents that day. He'd become a man with all the burdens, all the sorrows that entailed. A man within a boy's body, but still a man.

Which was why he had such a hard time in the system, a hard time trying to adjust to strangers, some of whom did their best to make him feel at home. Strangers who thought their rules applied to him. They didn't realize that it was too late for him. He didn't fit into a family structure anymore.

That door had closed for him when he was twelve.

He'd grown up isolated, insulated, not needing anyone or anything and not allowing anyone to need him.

So what was he doing here, letting this woman hang on to his hand as if it were her tether back to life as she waited for a resident doctor to examine her? Why wasn't he back at the apartment complex, taking down statements, doing his job? That was what he was good at—detective work, not comforting.

Hell, he wouldn't be able to comfort someone if his life depended on it. He just didn't know how. So there was absolutely no point in trying.

Yet Cavanaugh seemed glad to see him, glad to hang on to his hand as if it were some kind of talisman that could keep her safe. Her hand felt small within his. It made him want to protect her.

''You looked scared.'' He finally answered her earlier question.

He knew it wasn't the right thing to say, but it was why he was here. He saw no point in sugarcoating, or lying. He'd used lies to survive on the street when he'd run away from his last foster home. When he'd wound up living in an abandoned warehouse with another kid named Tierney. Used lies until the lines between reality and fantasy became completely blurred for him. He wasn't about to go there anymore. The path back always became hard to find.

Teri's first instinct was to say, no, she wasn't scared. The only thing that scared her was having harm come to the members of her family. Beyond that, she was pretty much fearless—like the rest of them.

But her reaction to hospitals, to what they represented to her, wasn't logical. It wasn't anything she wanted to explain to Hawk. "I don't expect you to understand."

The nurse had returned to take her pulse, then asked her a couple of quick questions, all of which went down on her chart. "How's the pain?" the woman asked.

"Not good," Teri muttered.

"This'll help."

Before she could ask what she was referring to, the nurse had given her an injection. Leaving to dispose of the needle, she returned with a starched hospital gown and deposited it on the bed.

"Here, put this on. Someone'll be here with you shortly." With that, the woman promptly disappeared again.

Teri pushed the gown onto the chair.

"What are you doing?" Hawk asked.

"There's no way I'm putting one of those things on. If they want to see this wound, all I have to do is lift up my shirt and they can cut away the bandages the paramedic put on." She saw he was about to say something and cut him off. "I won't be reduced to something sitting on an assembly line table."

Color rose to her cheeks. In the nine months they'd been partnered, he didn't remember ever seeing her get angry.

Or was that fear doing it to her? "Try me."

"Excuse me?"

"You said you didn't think I would understand why you're afraid of hospitals. Try me."

Even as the words came out of his mouth, he wasn't entirely sure just how they got there. He made his way through life not getting involved on any level with anything but the cases he was assigned, and then only in strictly a professional way. It was more than a matter of needing to be focused or possessing tunnel vision, he just didn't care to have people's lives touch his. It was cleaner that way. Neater.

Getting involved in someone's life wasn't worth the effort or the trouble. That, too, had been a lesson he'd gleaned while raising himself in his parents' run-down, rat-infested apartment.

Yet there was something about Cavanaugh that reached out to him.

Hawk was probably going to use this against her somehow, but since he asked, she felt she owed him an explanation. After all, he was still here, not turning his back and walking away.

"My uncle died in a hospital. This hospital," she added. "I was twelve."

Twelve.

The same age as he'd been when everything in his life had changed for him.

It felt odd having something beyond the police force in common with her. But then, having an uncle die in the line of duty wasn't exactly the same thing as seeing your parents gunned down in front of you for less money than some people spent for a week's groceries.

Restless, he shoved his hands into his pockets and wondered why he wasn't leaving. "You and your uncle were close?"

"Not as close as I am to my other uncle. Or my father," she added.

The time her father had been wounded in the line of duty, she thought her whole world had been shattering. She'd been so terrified, she couldn't get herself to come to the hospital with the rest of her siblings, afraid that if she did, if she came, it would be the last time she would see her father alive.

Just as it had been with her uncle.

"My whole family's close," she told him. Her words echoed back to her. Because he had no family, would he take that the wrong way? Would he think she was gloating because she had such a wonderful support system and he had no one to turn to?

Hawk made it seem as if he didn't need anyone, she reminded herself. He liked being alone.

Someone was paging a doctor to neurology. Hawk waited for the voice over the loudspeaker to fade away. "If you're so close, why didn't you want me to call one of them?"

"Because I don't want them to worry." She could almost envision the lot of them, crowding around the bed, shooting questions at her, looking like a backup for a worried Greek chorus. She could deal much better with them once she was completely patched up and this was behind her. "You, on the other hand, won't worry. You can just keep my mind off the fact that it hurts like a son of a gun."

His eyes narrowed. They both knew that she was responsible for ninety-nine percent of the conversations they did have. "And just how do you figure I'd do that?"

Teri grinned from ear to ear despite the pain that insisted on shooting through her with the precision of a Swiss watch. "Snappy patter comes to mind."

The remark was so incongruous, the image so out of character for him, Hawk laughed. The rich sound encompassed the tiny area they occupied.

She thought of her father's fresh coffee, first thing in the morning. Rich, smooth. Fortifying. "You know that's the first time I've ever heard you laugh. Nice. You should do that more often."

His face was somber again. "You do like telling people what to do, don't you?"

"Second nature, I guess." The pain had been melting away, but now the room was in danger of having the same thing happen to it. She grasped on to the metal railing on one side of the bed. "Damn, what did that nurse jab into me?"

"Well, if I'm lucky, something to put you to sleep." She began struggling to get off the bed. He caught her by the arm, holding her in place. "Hey, what the hell do you think you're doing?"

"I don't want to go to sleep here. I want to go

home.'' She was going to leave while she could still feel her legs. Sort of.

"Cavanaugh—"

She clutched his hand and raised imploring eyes up to his face. That was twice today she'd looked at him that way, and he didn't like it. Didn't like the position it put him in or how it made him feel—uncertain of his parameters around her. "Promise me that you'll take me home."

He'd seen prisoners less desperate to escape their jail cells. Hawk tried to remove her fingers and found that they were locked in almost a death grip around his wrist. Very firmly, he peeled back her fingers from his flesh. "Look, they have to stitch you up first, clean the wound—"

"Okay, okay," she interrupted, "but I'm not staying here overnight. Do you understand?"

What he understood was that somehow, the department had paired him with a woman who was a damn good detective, but that didn't change the fact that she was irritating and crazy to boot.

"If I say no, you're not going to let go of my hand, are you?"

He saw Teri slowly move her head from side to side and knew that she wasn't kidding. He could, of course, disengage himself from her. She had a good grip but she was, at bottom, absolutely no match for him. Even if he were a ninety-pound weakling, once the medication put her out, he could easily just slip away.

Again, he didn't know why he didn't. Maybe it was because for some reason she looked as if she needed him, and even though he told himself he didn't want to become involved, he had a hell of a hard time turning his back on that. On her.

It was why he was in law enforcement in the first place. Because people needed to be protected. From drug dealers, like the ones who had snuffed out his parents long before they were murdered, and from burglars, like the ones they'd caught today who had gotten off on seeing the terrified faces of their victims.

People needed protecting. And his badge made him a protector.

He sighed, surrendering the battle that had never really gotten onto the battlefield. "Okay, I'll stay."

"And take me home when the time comes."

"And take you home when the time comes," he finally said after she'd pinned him with those blue-gray eyes of hers.

It was another three hours before she was finally able to get into his car again. Three hours in which she'd been tortured, injected, stitched and finally bandaged. Three hours in which she'd hovered between pain and a drug-enabled euphoria.

She was still somewhere in the region of the latter. Stretching as best she could, she sighed and leaned back against the seat.

"God, I feel like I could just leap off the top of something and fly," she said.

Knowing that a silly grin had taken over her face, and not caring, Teri turned to flash it at her partner. She congratulated herself for finding a soft spot within his hard exterior. It made her feel giddy. She liked getting to him. Because he sure as hell had gotten to her.

Cavanaugh wasn't even attempting to put on her seat belt. Probably out of her head, Hawk decided. Reaching over her, he took hold of the seat belt and pulled it around her until he could fit the metal tongue into the groove and snap it in place.

"You feel that way because they pumped you full of Vicodin." He snapped his own seat belt into place, then looked at her. A tinge of amusement came out of nowhere and almost made him smile. She looked as if she didn't have a care in the world. "You don't have much tolerance for medication, do you?"

"Nope," she breathed, watching as the word floated away from her. She could almost see it. "But I can tolerate pain pretty well. And pain-in-the butts," she tacked on, looking at him significantly. Her grin widened, then narrowed as she attempted to pull thoughts together. It was like trying to corral six-week-old puppies in an open yard. "You know, you're a pretty nice guy when you let yourself."

Hawk began to thread his way out of the small side parking lot. He wasn't about to let her get sloppy on him. He was already having a hard enough time dealing with her and the strange undercurrent of feelings bubbling within him, as well. "You didn't leave me any choice."

"Oh, c'mon, Jackie, we both know better."

His spine stiffened at the sound of the name. He stepped a little too hard on the brake at the light. "Don't call me that."

His mother had called him Jackie when he was very, very young. Hearing the name set off chords he didn't want touched.

Her head spinning and bursts of joy throbbing through her veins, Teri backed off. "Sorry. 'Hawk' just seems too harsh for someone who held my hand."

"I didn't hold your hand, you held mine," he reminded her. It wasn't strictly true. He'd held hers while the doctor had stitched her up. "And it's Hawk. It always has been."

She sighed, cotton beginning to spread itself all around her as she sank back in the seat. The scenery was whizzing by her at a rate that made it hard for her to fully absorb. She still had trouble putting the sequence of events in order. Everything seemed to be vying for the same exact place. Holding her head didn't help. "My brain feels like mush."

He laughed under his breath. "And this is different from normal—how?"

Even in her present state of confusion, she was aware that he was trying to regain ground, trying to come off like the fire-breathing prince of darkness he always was. Too late.

"Sorry, I've seen your underbelly. You can't re-trace your steps."

She was babbling. It was probably the codeine the doctor had injected her with. But, God help him, she'd aroused his curiosity. "Retrace my steps? What are you talking about?"

"I'm on to you, Jack Hawkins. You come on like some Clint Eastwood knockoff, snapping out eight, nine words a day and keeping everyone at bay, but inside, you're a decent guy." She turned to look at him. "Just like your alter ego."

"What alter ego?" Bullet wound or no bullet wound, he was quickly losing his patience with her. "Cavanaugh, what the hell are you babbling about?"

It was as clear as a bell to her. "Clint Eastwood's a really nice guy when he's not playing tough guys. I heard somewhere that he's a real pussycat."

There was traffic on the road at this hour, which meant that he was stuck in the car even longer than he could tolerate. Served him right, he thought darkly. No good deed ever went unpunished.

"Cavanaugh, get this through your addled brain. I am not interested in your font of useless knowledge or your Vicodin-laced attempt at psychoanalysis. Now why don't you be a good little detective and just pass out the way the doctor said you would?"

"And make it easy for you?" she scoffed gleefully. "Nope. I want to enjoy this little breach." The sound of her own voice egged her on. "Don't get me wrong. I like tough guys. My cousin Patrick could spit nails—until his fiancée came into his life.'' And good luck to her, she thought. She adored her cousin, but living with him was going to be a tough thing. Patrick had his demons.

Not unlike the man next to her.

He had to stop her before she was off and running in another direction. He'd thought she was bad before, but that didn't hold a candle to the way she could run off at the mouth with this painkiller in her.

''Look, I don't know what gave you the idea that I'm interested in your family history, but I'm not, so save your breath.'' He glanced at her as he came to a light. She was smiling broadly at him. ''Now what?''

''It's not working.''

He knew he should just keep quiet. After all, that was his way, wasn't it? Allowing himself to enjoy silence? But something about the look on her face had him ask, ''What's not working?''

''Your tough-guy act. I've seen the light.''

He just bet she had. And it was probably all the shades of the rainbow. ''That's the pain medication. It distorts things.''

''Not enough to fool me.''

There was no point in arguing with her. He'd already learned that she could argue the ears off a stone statue.

''Look, Cavanaugh, just save your breath,'' he repeated. ''Okay?''

''Okay.''

He'd won that round. Hawk found that difficult to believe. She never retreated like that. It wasn't like her. As he came to a stop before another light, wondering if she was all right, Hawk looked at her.

The next thing he knew, Teri was kissing him.

Chapter Four

It just happened. She hadn't planned it, or even thought it out.

To say she had never thought about kissing Hawk would have been a lie. She had. Several times. The man was tall, dark and handsome by absolutely anyone's standards. But she wasn't really attracted to him, she'd insisted. Brooding men weren't her type. She liked outgoing, gregarious men. Men who knew how to have fun and didn't mean anything by it once the good times were over.

Simple. That was the way she liked it.

Jack Hawkins, on the other hand, just breathed complexity. Every word he uttered—when he deigned to utter any—all but screamed the word.

No, she wasn't attracted to him. Nope, not a whit.

If anything, Hawk was her pet project. She meant to drag her partner out among the living if it was the last thing she did on this earth. She had to get him to loosen up and smile more than once every nine, ten months or so. Nothing else, just that.

Kissing him hadn't been a means to that goal.

What had brought her today to this junction of skin pressed against skin was extreme gratitude, or at least that was the excuse she fed herself. Hawk had remained by her side at the hospital when she knew every single inclination inside his body leaned toward walking away. That he didn't meant a great deal to her.

So she was kissing him because she was filled with gratitude. Gratitude and a healthy dose of Vicodin, or whatever painkiller the nurse had injected into her.

And maybe it was the Vicodin spiking up through her system, but suddenly, the outside world faded away. The wound, the traffic, the car itself that Hawk was driving—all melted into oblivion as she became aware of this intense rise of heat all around her. Not like when she'd gotten shot and yet, somehow oddly similar.

Except without the pain.

No matter which way you sliced it, Teri felt she was definitely having an out-of-body experience and not really minding it one bit.

What the hell was going on here? Always aware

of his surroundings, Hawk had not seen this coming. Not in his wildest dreams. Not Cavanaugh.

It wasn't even as if they had particularly easy access to one another and her lips had accidentally bumped against his. The car had bucket seats, for Pete's sake.

One hand on the wheel, he grabbed Teri by the shoulder with his other for the purpose of removing her mouth from his. He was as surprised as anyone when he found himself holding on to her instead.

Surprise very quickly turned into something that involved not just his brain but his whole body. Desire moved through it like a sleeping snake uncoiling itself after an aeon of inactivity.

Worse still, Hawk could feel himself reacting to her in ways he didn't welcome. Sure, the woman was attractive—anyone with eyes could readily see that. But she was also a walking mouth, someone who never knew when to cease and desist—which for him would have been before the very first word was uttered. As it was, Cavanaugh had more words in her arsenal than could be found within the pages of a congressional investigation.

So why the hell did he feel as if someone had just knocked him off his feet by swinging a wrecking ball into him?

The sound of horns blaring directly behind his vehicle pulled Hawk out of the center of the vortex he found himself in and pushed him quickly back out into the real world.

Finally wedging a space between them, he turned and quickly clamped both hands firmly on the steering wheel before he was tempted to repeat the offense.

Before he was tempted to initiate the next kiss himself.

The woman tasted sweeter than anything he'd ever had.

The moment his eyes were back in focus, Hawk took his foot off the brake and stepped down on the gas pedal.

Hard.

They flew through the intersection.

He realized that they'd come extremely close to having an accident. It would have taken very little for his foot to have slipped off the brake while his attention had been directed to other regions. Although there was no car in front of them, there *was* an intersection. They could have been smack in the middle of it with through traffic slamming into them before his brain would have registered the danger.

That had never happened to him before.

His pulse was racing harder than if he'd just done a 10K run.

Once they were on the other side of the intersection, he glared at her. She'd made him lose control and he didn't like that. It didn't go with the image he had of himself.

"What the hell was that?"

Teri took a deep breath. It didn't help. Her heart was pounding harder than a drum soloist showing off his expertise. She took another breath before slanting her eyes in his direction. "Boy, you *do* need to get out more. That's commonly known as a kiss."

If he clenched the steering wheel any harder, he had a feeling it would shatter. "I know what the hell it is, I want to know why it was coming from you."

She'd come on to him, she realized. Oh, God, how had that happened? What was she acting on? Did she really feel that attracted to him? No, it was the medication—that's what it was—taking away the restraints, the walls. Her judgment. Her mind fuzzy, she searched for something plausible to use as an excuse. "I kiss, Hawk. I kiss a lot. Don't look so uneasy. A kiss isn't always a prelude to sex—"

"I wasn't uneasy," he snapped. The next moment, he got himself under control. It was a lie. He was uneasy and he had no idea *why* he was uneasy, why his nerves felt as if they were being pulled apart, which just made the situation that much more irritating. "And before you and I have sex, hell will be selling overcoats."

"Charmingly put," she said. He probably had no idea that if she hadn't had a healthy self-esteem, that would have gone a long way toward destroying it. "Have I told you how great you are for my ego?"

Hawk snorted. She was the last person who needed to be treated with verbal kid gloves. "You don't need me for your ego. You've got other guys for that, hanging around like mindless flies."

She shook her head, then regretted it. The inside

of the car spun a little. "Honey, pure honey on that tongue of yours." And then she smiled. Well, well, well, he was aware of other men looking at her. Interesting. "So you do notice things sometimes."

"I'm a detective. I'm supposed to notice things."

"You don't notice the women drooling after you."

There she went, exaggerating again. "Nobody's drooling," he heard himself snap.

Damn it, Cavanaugh was doing it to him again, making him lose his cool, his control. How did she manage to do that when he usually could keep such tight rein on what was happening inside of him? And why did he have to be partnered with her in the first place?

He realized that she still hadn't answered his question to his satisfaction. "Why did you kiss me?"

His profile was rigid. It was the kind of profile, she caught herself thinking, that could have easily been chiseled in rock. No soft edges, no curves, just planes and angles. A born tough guy. "Just the facts, ma'am,' right?"

"What?"

"Joe Friday. *Dragnet,*" she said.

She could see that the names of the program and its chief character meant nothing to Hawk. The man needed color in his life. Broad strokes. She had a feeling his life was done in fine-point pencil.

He sure didn't kiss that way, a small voice from the inside of her ebbed delirium whispered.

Teri made the only assumption she could. "I take

it you weren't raised on police dramas the way I was.''

A great many of the programs had come via cable channels that featured old series from bygone eras. She could remember watching them, sitting on the floor in front of her father's chair. Once in a while, when police work allowed, he was even in the chair, explaining things to her. Her desire to be a police detective had come just as much from those programs as it had from wanting to emulate her father, to give her something in common with him.

No, he thought, he wasn't raised on watching police dramas, he *lived* police dramas. He'd lost count the number of times the police had come knocking on his parents' door. A good many times they'd been arrested. He'd watched it all from the closet where his mother made him hide so that social services wouldn't come to take him away. The way they had the day his parents were murdered.

He shook his mind free of the memories and shot Teri a look. "You're changing the subject, Cavanaugh. Again.''

"No, I'm embellishing on the subject,'' she corrected. "Otherwise, everyone talks like you.''

At least then, people would get to the point once in a while. "Not a bad thing.''

Now they were on a topic near and dear to her heart. With only two thirds of her mental firing pins in order, she warmed up to the subject. "It is for communication. Nuances are what tell us things about people.''

"Maybe I don't want people knowing anything about me.''

"Sorry, Hawk. This is the Internet age. If you can't get information about someone one way, you can get it another. In the end, there is no mystery.'' He had a very odd look on his face. "Except maybe for what you're thinking about right now.''

Finally, they'd reached her housing development. He'd begun to feel as if it was an endless journey and he was stuck making it with her droning on in his ear. Hawk spared her a look as he drove through the entrance. "You're better off not knowing what I'm thinking now.''

She was suddenly beginning to feel very, very tired. That, she assumed, was undoubtedly the effects of the medication she'd been injected with. She had to admit she liked the high she'd had just moments ago. Liked, too, the sensation that had permeated her body when she'd kissed him.

Liked it a lot.

Liked it better than matching wits with him.

Okay, it was time to stop yanking his chain. "I kissed you to say thank you. It really is as simple as that,'' Teri told him.

Stirring him up was not a way to say thank you, he thought. "A handshake would have done.'' And left him a great deal less unsettled, he added silently.

She smiled. It hit him right between the eyes. "Not this time."

"Say thank you for what?"

He didn't even realize what he'd done, did he? That was so typical of him. When it came to complexity, it only involved him. The rest of the world he seemed to view in terms of black and white. She wondered which side he placed her on.

"You stayed with me at the hospital, when I knew you would have rather hit the street again." Because she'd asked him to, he had stayed even while the emergency room physician had removed the bullet fragment from her side and had stitched her up. She'd held his hand throughout the whole ordeal, and at times she could feel the probing scalpel, feel the needle despite the injections she'd been given to mute the pain. Hawk had never once given any indication that she'd channeled the pain and squeezed his hand far too hard.

Hawk dismissed her gratitude as unnecessary. "You had a vise lock on my hand. I figured if I made any sudden moves, you would have ripped out my shoulder."

"Not hardly."

Something inside of her wanted to kiss him again. Even as the last effects of the painkiller were fading. But because there was no medication to blame it on, she banked the urge down.

It took her a moment to realize that the car had stopped moving.

"We're here," Hawk told her when she made no move to unbuckle her belt and open the door. Why wasn't she getting out? Was she weak? He knew she should have stayed in the hospital overnight for observation. The woman didn't have the sense of a three-minute-old butterfly.

She took a breath, bracing herself, hoping she wouldn't embarrass herself when she tried to get out. "Yeah, we are."

He needed to get back. He was primary on this investigation and that meant not letting the lead fall into a subordinate's hands.

But he never liked leaving anything half done. That included shepherding a wounded partner home. "You want me to come inside with you?"

She *was* embarrassing herself and she hadn't even taken a step out of the car yet. She didn't like appearing like a weakling. "No, I'll be all right." She looked at him significantly. "You've done enough penance for one day."

"I wouldn't exactly call it penance," he muttered, then allowed a slight smile to take possession of his mouth when she looked at him in abject surprise. "But close."

He watched her begin to unbuckle her seat belt, then saw the way she winced. Her wound had to be hurting her like hell. The painkiller must be wearing off by now.

"That's going to be tender for a while," he told

her. Moving her hands out of the way, Hawk un-buckled her seat belt for her.

As his hands brushed against hers, her eyes met his. "What would you know about tender?"

It was a loaded question and she knew it, but maybe because, for a fleeting second, she'd come face-to-face with her own mortality, she was feeling a little more reckless today than was her norm.

"I've caught a couple of bullets," he answered.

She knew about that, that he'd caught one to the shoulder in his rookie year and another just above his heart a couple of years ago. In both cases, he'd been lucky. Nothing vital had been injured.

But that wasn't what she meant. "I wasn't talking about body pain."

The late-afternoon March sun filled the interior of the Crown Victoria, making it warmer than the temperature right outside the windows. Sunbeams got tangled in her hair.

Hawk looked at her for a long moment. Something tightened in the middle of his gut, fueled by the sharp urge that kept insistently reappearing each time he banked it down.

He pushed it away again.

They were partners and while he didn't exactly relish their partnership, he had to admit Cavanaugh was a good cop—good at her job and honest. That counted for a lot. He didn't really like having to work with anyone, but he supposed she was better than most.

Kissing her, making the first move himself this

time, would place everything they had so far into severe jeopardy.

"Guess I don't know anything at all about it," he finally said.

Yeah, he did, but she'd let him have the lie if it made him feel better. This was something she wasn't up to exploring right now. Not when her brain felt like warm Swiss cheese.

"Didn't think so."

Turning away from him, she started to get out.

He had a feeling if he let her out of the car on her own, she was going to fall flat on her face. Stifling a sigh, Hawk opened the door on his side, got out and rounded the hood. By the time she'd swung out her legs, he was there, waiting to take her arm.

"I'm not an invalid, Hawk."

If she meant to make him back away, she was going to have to do better than that. He held on to her arm, choreographing her steps to the house. "You pushed me out of the way and got shot yourself, then refused to stay overnight in the hospital, signing out against the doctor's orders. I think the *I* word we're looking for here is *idiot*, not *invalid*."

She was beginning to get a handle on him. He became gruffer whenever he did a good deed and seemed to be approaching decent human behavior. She held on to him a little more than she was happy about, trying to placate her self-disgust by reminding herself that she was still pumped full of medication, even if she didn't feel it in a good way anymore.

"Good thing you didn't become a doctor. Your bedside manner is really lousy."

He brought her to the door, trusting that she would rather go inside on her own power. Besides, he had no desire to run into any of the other Cavanaughs and be detained for questioning. Relating what happened was up to her. He disengaged himself from her. "Then I'd better get going."

But as he turned to walk away, she called after him. "Hawk?"

"What?" Impatience hummed around the single word.

"Thanks again."

He paused, then nodded. If not for her quick action, their positions might have been reversed right now. He wasn't about to forget that soon. "Yeah, me, too."

Turning away, Teri smiled as she let herself into the house. With an annoyingly wobbly, uncertain gait, she headed straight for the stairs and to her room. Any excess strength she had faded the moment she saw her bed. Falling onto it, she was out within three minutes.

It didn't even occur to her until later that day that she hadn't seen her father's white car parked in the driveway.

The last person he expected to see walking into the office the following morning came breezing in a few minutes before nine. Hawk put down the statements he'd taken from the victim late yesterday afternoon.

Frowning, he was on his feet in less time than it took her to cross the threshold.

"What the hell are you doing here?"

Ah, she thought, the dulcet sounds of harmonious camaraderie.

"I work here, remember?" Teri looked to the far end where her desk was butted up against his. "Or did you give my desk away already?"

Why did he expect normal behavior from someone who wasn't normal? "You were shot. You're supposed to take a few days off to rest."

Masking the toll the effort took, she moved past Hawk at a good clip. Her side was hurting today worse than it had yesterday, but she needed to get her mind off the pain and do something other than watch television. Tomorrow, she promised herself, would be better. All she had to do was get past today.

"It's a cinch you've never been to my house. You can't rest when you have a fifty-five-year-old man fussing over you." Reaching her desk, she deliberately didn't sink down in her chair. She refused to display any signs of weakness in front of Hawk. He'd only use it against her. "This morning, he was coming up with alternate law enforcement careers that would keep me behind a desk."

"What were they?"

He sounded far too interested and she knew he wasn't thinking of himself. She waved away his question. "Never mind. I love what I do and I'm here."

She nodded as Mulrooney got up from his chair and crossed to her.

"Welcome back." He gave her a bear hug. "You okay to be here?"

"Never better." She managed to get the remark out without gritting her teeth together. She looked from one man to the other. "Did we get anything out of those guys we caught yesterday?"

Disgust covered Dan Mulrooney's broad, florid face. "They clammed up and demanded to talk to a lawyer."

She made the natural assumption. "Public defender?" The men looked like two-bit thugs.

"No, some pricey guy." She could see that Mulrooney had been as surprised by the piece of information as she was. "Your cousin Janelle was by. Said she'd heard of him."

"Where do two-bit burglars get the money for a pricey lawyer?" Teri wanted to know.

It was a rhetorical question. She didn't expect to get an answer. But Hawk had been chewing on the same question all evening. "Maybe they're not working alone but for someone."

She caught his wavelength and was off and running, charging her words with all the enthusiasm he lacked. "Someone who can afford it." Her eyes were positively glowing. She loved when one thing hooked up to another. "Someone big." She grinned at Hawk. "You know, you don't talk much, but when you do, it's worth listening to."

"Unlike some people," he said under his breath. He was angry about her being back so soon. Angry that she was risking her health. And angry that what she did got under his skin the way it did.

She was back, Teri thought, finally lowering herself into her chair.

And it felt good.

Chapter Five

Teri stopped dead.

Behind her, the ladies' room door she'd just come through lightly tapped her as it swung back into place, nudging her out of her trance. Feeling a little woozy, she'd gone in for a couple of minutes respite without several sets of male eyes watching her, most notably Hawk's. She'd had the feeling all day that he'd been waiting for her to pass out, or visibly droop.

Which was a great incentive to keep pushing.

But she hadn't expected to be waylaid by the sudden appearance of her father walking along on what she deemed now to be her turf.

"Dad, what are you doing here?"

Her eyes narrowed as she crossed to him. Granted,

this whole building had once been her father's domain and she knew he had to miss being here, had to miss being the chief of what had become a damn fine police force. But the first reason that occurred to her for his presence had nothing to do with his having a bout of nostalgia, or meeting up with old friends. It was far more personal than that. And very typical. Since Rose Cavanaugh had disappeared out of their lives, he had transformed from a parent to both mother and father to all of them.

"You're not checking up on me, are you?"

So engrossed in thought, Andrew had all but walked into his daughter. If anything, he knew he had to look more surprised to see her than she him.

Forcing a smile to his lips, he shook his head. "Hell, no. I know better than that." And then he deadpanned with a wink. "I've got my spies doing that for me."

With her father, it wasn't always easy to know when he was kidding. And she wouldn't put it past him to have one of his old friends look in on her and then call in with a report. He was like that, letting them independently go their own way and fly high. All the while he secretly held up a net to catch them in case they should fall.

She scrutinized his face. At least the worried frown wasn't there anymore, the way it had been yesterday when her father had come home to find her there ahead of him. He'd tried every argument in the book to get her to take a sick day today and rest, but the more he pushed, the more she'd dug in. She supposed that maybe she did possess a little of that superhero complex that Hawk had accused her of having, but that wasn't anything she was willing to own up to out loud.

She hooked her arm through her father's, taking comfort in his strength. Not a day went by when she wasn't proud to be Andrew Cavanaugh's daughter.

"So, what does bring you here?" she asked cheerfully. "Catching up on stories with the guys?"

He didn't like lying, especially to his children, but agreeing to the scenario Teri had just provided him with was a lot easier than going into an explanation of what he was really doing here. He'd come to bring to the crime lab the spoon he'd lifted from the diner. He wanted the head tech to match the fingerprints on it against the prints he knew had to be all over the well-worn, much-read copy of Rose's favorite book, *Gone with the Wind.* How many times had he teased her that she cared more for Rhett Butler than she did for him? Her answer had always been the same. That until the day that Rhett did come along, he'd do just fine.

The argument the day she had driven out of his life was that he was afraid that "Rhett" had come—in the guise of his brother Mike. It had been a stupid, stupid argument, and one of the very few times he'd allowed jealousy to get the better of him. And he'd been paying for that stupidity for the past fifteen years of his life.

He knew how his children felt about his ongoing search for their mother. They thought he was knocking his head against a stone wall. He'd noticed the look of pity in their eyes every time they saw him opening up the folders and spreading them out on his desk.

"Give it up, Dad," even Rayne, his youngest, had begged him. Rayne, who had taken her mother's disappearance the hardest and who, after all these years, had finally come around and accepted the fact that her mother was gone, the way the rest of them had.

Except that he knew his wife wasn't gone. He'd seen her, talked to her. And now he needed proof.

"Something like that," he allowed, making his decision.

Had he said the words to Callie, he knew that she'd be all over him, examining his tone, his inflection, the look on his face as he said what he said. His oldest daughter was part mind reader. But Teri was his firecracker. Hardly one thought fully formed in her mind before she was on to another.

He figured he was safe.

Andrew looked at his daughter more closely as they walked slowly to the squad room. She still looked too pale. But she was twenty-seven and he couldn't very well lock her in her room. "So, how's your day going?"

"Not too well." She struggled to bank down her growing frustration. They were close, so close. "We can't get anything out of the 'suspects' we caught yesterday. They've lawyered up. But the M.O. is an exact duplicate of the other four home invasions that've gone down in the past month. The burglars got in using a key. The people are all upscale, but other than that, they have nothing in common except that they were targeted by these creeps.''

"Keep at it, Teri. You'll find the answer. You always do.'' Afraid she might redirect the conversation back to him, Andrew drew his arm away from hers and glanced at his watch. "Well, don't let me keep you from your work. And try to get home at a decent hour tonight.''

It was her turn to wink at him. "That all depends on what you mean by decent.'' Moving away, she began to disappear around the corner.

Teri was his night owl, given to partying almost as hard as she was to devoting herself to police work. "Sometime before dawn,'' he called after her.

Her voice came floating back. "You got it.''

Shaking his head, Andrew hurried off to the stairwell. It was the safest route right now. He didn't want to take a chance on running into another one of his children. All five worked here, not to mention his four nephews. Even Janelle, Brian's girl, was wont to pop up here, working with the detectives in her capacity as assistant district attorney.

And although his late brother, Mike's daughter Patience had opted for a different path by becoming a veterinarian, her services were frequently used in providing medical care for the force's K-9 squad. That meant he could run into her, too. He didn't feel like having to field questions from her, either, although of the lot of them, Patience was the most unassuming and laid-back.

The stairwell was definitely the way to go until he was ready to share whatever findings Claude Wilkins came up with at the lab. Wilkins owed him more than a few favors, not the least of which was his present position as head of the crime lab. He'd promised to get the results to him as quickly as possible.

Until then, he'd keep his own counsel. There was no use in stirring everyone up if there was no match.

But in his heart, he knew there would be.

His footsteps echoed as he went down the metal steps.

"Hey, Cavanaugh, I saw your dad here earlier." Mulrooney sat down at his desk, momentarily tearing his attention away from the slightly squished package of Ding Dongs that he'd ransomed out of the vending machine. It was his third such venture today. He claimed that chocolate made him think more clearly.

Teri didn't look up from the notes she was studying. So far, the flow chart she'd put together of all the victims had yielded nothing even vaguely enlightening. "Yeah, me, too," she muttered.

"What's your dad doing hanging around the crime lab?"

Mulrooney's innocent question, uttered as he sank his teeth into the plastic wrapper and yanked, speared through her thoughts. Her head jerked up in his direction as he got her full attention.

"The crime lab?"

"Yeah." The older detective shook his bounty out of its plastic confines onto a sheet of white paper on his desk. "Saw him giving something to Wilkins. A spoon and a book of some kind." Using a plastic knife he kept in his desk, he meticulously divided the dessert into halves. "He doing consulting work for the department or something these days? I mean, the man was damn good when he worked here." There was a fond note in his voice. "Everything ran like a well-oiled machine and crimes were down while number of cases solved were up." Picking up the first half of the treat, he prepared to pop the whole thing into his mouth. "Maybe you can have him wander in and solve this case for us. You know, lay hands on the files and come up with an answer." The suggestion was followed by a chuckle.

Teri chewed on her lip, thinking. Her father hadn't mentioned anything about stopping at the crime lab when she'd run into him. Now that she thought about it, he looked unwilling to talk about being here at all. And why would he be giving Wilkins a spoon and a book? Something was definitely up.

More than anything else, she hated not knowing what was going on.

She reached for the telephone on her desk, intending to call home and get to the bottom of this. But before she could dial, Hawk was standing next to her, putting several sheets on her desk.

"What's this?" she asked.

"Found another home invasion, sloppier than the others. Timeline puts it first." Suddenly aware that there didn't seem to be enough space between them, Hawk took a step back. "Maybe there was a learning curve for our guys."

Teri scanned the papers he'd printed up. "What do you mean?"

Their desks were butted up against one another, head to head. He sat down behind his, allowing her to absorb what he was saying. Finding himself getting more and more in tune to her, he noticed she looked a little distracted. "The crime lab boys found prints on the scene that didn't belong to any of the family members or friends."

Adrenaline surged through her. "Did the prints match anyone in the system?"

His expression never changed. But then, Teri had a feeling he could have discovered gold on his property and never bat an eyelash. "No, but neither 'suspect' has any priors."

At least this was possible progress. "Okay—" she pushed back from her desk and stood "—then let's go and see if we can get ourselves a match."

There was no match.

The prints that were on file from the Del Torro case didn't match the prints of either of the two men who

MARIE FERRARELLA   79

had been captured invading the Wong apartment the day before.

"Only means that there's probably more people involved than the ones we've got cooling their heels in lockup," Teri theorized with a deep sigh. "But then we already figured this operation has to be bigger than Tweedledum and Tweedledee."

Still, it irritated her to move forward only to slide back again like this. She wanted that burst, the lead that finally brought all the pieces together.

She paused, holding the results that had just been spit out of the machine. Another question nagged at her. Maybe she could at least get the answer and put it to rest. "Claude, what did my father give you earlier today?"

Already at the door, Hawk turned slowly around to listen to the head technician's reply. When she glanced in her partner's direction, he was watching her, not Wilkins. She shut him out.

Wilkins, a bewhiskered man in his fifties, measured his words out as slowly as he did the evidence he examined. "He wanted a favor."

"What kind of a favor?"

To her frustration, Wilkins shook his head as he turned back to his work. "Look, Teri, I'm not comfortable talking about it. If you want to know, why don't you ask him yourself?"

"I will." Banking down her annoyance, she turned on her heel and walked out.

Hawk matched his stride to hers. For a small

woman, she could cover a lot of ground when she put her mind to it.

"We're working on a case, Cavanaugh."

So now he was her conscience as well as her partner? "I know," she snapped, pushing the down button on the elevator pad. "I don't need you to tell me that."

Her tone didn't put him off. His own was infuriatingly mild as he continued. "Don't you think that should be your first priority?"

The elevator arrived and she stomped in, punching the button for the floor she wanted before she trusted herself to answer. "My family's my first priority. My job's a close second."

He stood beside her, the six-foot-two voice of reason she didn't want to hear right now. "Seems to me if your father wanted you to know, he would have told you when you ran into him."

So he'd overheard Mulrooney earlier. She resented him taking this high-handed attitude about her life. "What are you, an authority on father-daughter relationships all of a sudden?"

His shoulders rose and fell in a seemingly disinterested shrug. "Just making an observation."

"Well, don't."

Arriving on their floor, she got out ahead of him. But two steps toward the squad room, she got a renewed hold over her emotions. Since yesterday, they seemed to be all over the place. Maybe getting shot had affected her more than she realized. She definitely had to get a grip.

"Sorry," she apologized. "I didn't mean to get so testy. It's just that—"

"You have to know everything."

Mentally, she counted to ten. She couldn't follow an apology with an explosion. "Not everything, just what's going on with my family. With my father," she underscored. Because without him, there would have been no family. Andrew Cavanaugh was the glue that held all of them together.

"Have you ever heard of privacy?"

"I have." Was he bent on getting her angry, or didn't he realize how annoying his questions, his quiet tone were? "I've got no intentions of posting my findings on the Internet." She stopped walking, choosing instead to have it out with him in an alcove of the hallway. "Look, in my house, we care about the other person, and if there's something going on, we all pitch in to work it out. My father deliberately held back when I asked him what he was doing here."

Hawk could always see things from the point of view of the loner. And right now, it appeared that for all his gregariousness, Andrew Cavanaugh had assumed the role of the loner.

"Maybe he had his reasons." He looked at her pointedly. "And whatever they are, they don't include you."

Her temper flared again. "Caring always includes me. That's just how it is."

"He's a big boy." Because standing here in this small, recessed space in the hall with her was affecting him in a manner he didn't welcome, Hawk backed out, signaling an end to the dialogue. Convincing Cavanaugh of something when she didn't want to hear it was like trying to pour water into a stone. "When he's ready for you to know, he'll tell you. Meanwhile, don't let it eat you up. You want to do some investigating, save it for the job."

Teri watched his back as he walked away from her. She frowned. Hawk was right. She didn't want to give it to him, but he was. If her father was being secretive, it was for a reason. Most likely, he probably thought he was shielding them from something.

For now she'd let the matter go. But not for long.

Wilkins called later to say that none of the DNA evidence that had been collected from the any of the other four invasions matched the DNA of the two men they had in custody.

"Damn."

It took effort not to slam down the phone. This latest dead end sapped away the last bit of her already-dwindling energy. Dragging a hand through her hair, Teri made up her mind. She knew she wasn't going to be any good to the case unless she got away from it for a while.

Hitting the right combination of keys, she shut off

MARIE FERRARELLA   83

her computer. Her shift had been over for more than an hour. It was time to go home.

"There's no match."

Not raising his eyes from his work, Hawk said, "I gathered."

"I'm calling it a night." Hawk barely nodded to acknowledge hearing the information. Ready to dash out, Teri lingered for a moment. Everyone else had already checked out for the night. She'd hung around waiting for Wilkins. God knew why Hawk was hanging around. "I'm stopping at the Shannon, want to come along?"

Hawk looked up from his notes. Cavanaugh had invited him to the local police hangout a number of times and he'd never taken her up on it, preferring his own company and the soothing dim atmosphere of the bar near his studio apartment.

To call Joe's a dingy dive was being charitable. As far as drink or food went, the Shannon undoubtedly had it all over Joe's. Still, the people who frequented Joe's valued their anonymity and respected the same of others. He didn't have to talk if he didn't want to. That had always been a selling feature for him.

"Got my own place to go."

It was a dismissal. But tonight, she didn't feel like being dismissed. Coming around to his desk, she leaned over until she was almost in his face. "I owe you a drink for yesterday."

Because she was far too close into his comfort zone for him to think clearly, he pushed his chair back.

Giving himself some breathing space. "You took my bullet. I'd say it was even."

"Damn it, Hawk, just come out for a drink with me." Determined, Teri planted herself on his desk, blocking any view he had of the file he'd been studying. "I promise I won't bite."

He looked at her for a long moment, remembering the short, blood-heating interlude in the car yesterday afternoon. Remembering the taste of her lips against his. Remembering, too, other things that had gone on. No, he wouldn't say she didn't bite. Or at the very least, she had a really big kick to her.

Very slowly, what could have passed for a smile in some circles rose to his lips, curving them just a hint. "Can I have that in writing?"

She caught his drift immediately. "If you mean yesterday, I wasn't biting. That was called a kiss and you really do need to get out more."

So she'd already said. He had no idea what made him ask the next question. "Why? For lessons?"

"Nope, that is one thing you don't need, Hawkins. Lessons." Even as she spoke, a glimmer of the feeling she'd experienced yesterday came back to her. She knew enough to be able to separate it from the half-drowsy state created by the painkillers she'd taken. His kiss had curled her toes. "I'd even go so far as to say that you were a natural."

He tugged on the folder that was now partially planted beneath her butt. "Then I don't need to get out more, do I?"

He'd trapped her with her own words, but she wasn't one to accept defeat easily. Rather than move as he tugged, she took hold of his sleeve and tugged herself.

"Come with me to the Shannon or I'll come into the squad room tomorrow morning and tell everyone that you carried me down five flights of stairs and held my hand while the surgeon stitched me up."

Obviously her perspective had gotten confused. "I didn't hold your hand—you held on to mine. I just didn't relish the idea of having it ripped out of the socket, remember?"

After twenty-four hours, you'd think he would have come up with a better excuse than that, she thought. He'd stayed because he'd wanted to stay, pure and simple. If he hadn't, no power on earth would have made him.

Just like now. Teri scooted off the desk and crossed to the door. "Your whole reputation as a tough guy is on the line here," she warned, her hand on the doorknob.

"No one would believe you." He was already going back to his work.

Teri cocked her head, looking at him. Waiting. "You want to take that chance?"

He wasn't going to get anywhere further tonight. His brain felt tired and he needed a respite. Looking up, he saw her still standing there. Hawk frowned. "Just one drink?"

She raised her right hand as if she was about to

take a solemn oath. "Just one drink. Unless, of course, you want more."

Maybe, a small voice whispered within him. Annoyed, he blocked it out. "I want less," he informed her.

"Then one it is." The bar, run by two brothers who were both former policemen, was located several blocks away from the police precinct. "C'mon, we'll take my car. I'll drive."

Hawk rose to his feet. "We'll take both cars and we'll both drive."

He didn't trust her further than he could throw her. Less, he amended. If he gave her an inch, she'd take a mile. And he might just let her. That would lead to places neither one of them could afford to go.

It didn't take a clairvoyant to know what he was thinking. She smiled at him. "Looking to make a quick getaway?"

Slipping on his jacket, he gave her a dark look. "I don't appreciate you constantly second-guessing what's on my mind. Stop it."

"Yes, sir." She'd won the round, she could afford to be generous. And then she added with a grin, "You never know when that might come in handy someday."

He didn't see how that was possible.

The wall of noise within the Shannon died down several decibels the moment he walked in behind Teri. His first inclination was just to back out, get back into his car and go to Joe's. He hadn't wanted to come anyway. It wasn't as if he didn't see enough of the others, especially Cavanaugh, during regular hours.

But he'd never backed away from anything and this little venture fell under the heading of a challenge, no matter how small.

So he kept on walking, his eyes fixed on the long, sleek bar that ran the length of the rear wall. How long could it take to drink one beer?

Chapter Six

Hawk frowned. It was taking far too long to down this one beer. Every time he bent his elbow, about to drink some more of the deep amber liquid, someone else would come up to bend his ear instead.

If he didn't know any better, he would have said that the whole establishment had been packed with people who belonged to T.A.—Teris Anonymous, there to try to purge as many words out of their system as was humanly possible without imploding.

It was his idea of a living hell, being surrounded by an endless supply of people who did nothing but talk. And talk. And talk.

Even people he thought kept mostly their own council, like his partner's older brother, Shaw, couldn't seem to pass up the opportunity to stop by and say something to him tonight.

In Shaw's case, it was advice. The tall, muscular detective took a chair next to him at the small table Teri had staked out for them while her older sister, Callie, flanked him on the other side. He was getting a triple dose of Cavanaughs, the only saving grace being that the older two didn't talk nearly as much as his partner did.

Straddling his chair cowboy fashion, Shaw took a healthy swig from his mug before saying, "You've got my sincere pity, Hawk."

With a lead-in like that, Hawk supposed he was expected to bite, so to save time, he did. "And why's that?"

"Being partnered with Teri." He nodded toward his middle sister, who had temporarily gotten up to say something to one of the other detectives. "She's relentless. I'm pretty convinced that she could get Satan to do her bidding if she kept after him long enough."

Hawk couldn't help wondering if the other detective was somehow making a comparison here, equating him to the prince of darkness. The thought amused him. It wouldn't be the first time he'd been thought to walk on the dark side.

Which was fine with him. The less people knew about him, the better. He didn't particularly like the idea of his life being up for public viewing. He was an honest cop—that was all anyone needed to know about him. Anything else was no one's business but his.

"Good to know," Hawk murmured. He took the momentarily lull to finally drain the last of his beer. It was way past time to go.

Out of the corner of his eye, he saw Teri on her way back. For a moment, he watched as her hips gently swayed with every step she took. And then he realized she was motioning to the bartender to send over one more beer, pointing to him as the recipient.

Hawk set his mug firmly on the table. "You said one," he told her as she rejoined them.

Callie looked from her sister to Teri's partner. "One doesn't really mean one."

Was this one going to be as irritating as her sister? Hawk wondered. "It does in my book."

Looking at Callie, Teri shrugged. "He follows a straight and narrow path." With a wave of her hand to the bartender, she canceled the new order.

She was disappointed, but a deal was a deal, even if it hadn't turned out the way she'd wanted. She'd hoped that since he'd finally joined her for a sociable drink, she could get Hawk to come around, to open up—at least just a tiny bit.

Although he seemed to get along well enough with Shaw and Callie, as always, Hawk seemed to prefer to sit back and listen. Or least give the appearance of listening. With Hawk, you could never tell if he was taking everything in or if he was off somewhere else entirely in his head.

She wondered why he was content to be alone. She wouldn't have been able to stand it. There was so much you missed that way.

Teri looked at the empty mug, knowing he was about to leave. "Doesn't seem like nearly enough to say thanks," she told him.

He hadn't come here so that she could say thanks. He'd come because…well, he wasn't really sure why he'd come now that he thought about it. Maybe it had been his attempt at shutting her up so that he wouldn't have to hear her invite him here anymore.

Even as he formed the thought, he knew it was a lie. Nothing could shut Cavanaugh up for long, and after nine months, he'd be the first to testify to that.

He shrugged noncommittally. "Like I said, one canceled out the other."

Teri studied him for a moment, temporarily ignoring the fact that they weren't alone, that there was more than a score of ears within hearing distance. "Then why did you come?"

He gave her the excuse that came up most readily. "Because you wouldn't stop pushing until I gave in. Now you'll stop."

Shaw laughed, shaking his head. "You don't know her very well yet, do you? You gave in to her. Refueled by her triumph, she'll just push more. It's the nature of the beast." Teri swatted at Shaw. He ducked a beat too late. Her fingertips made contact with the back of his head. "Emphasis on *beast*," Shaw added, ducking before she could make contact this time around. He pretended to eye his middle sister. "Dangerous thing, the department giving her a gun. But then, if they gave one to Rayne, I guess they'd issue a weapon to just about anyone."

"Hair-trigger temper?" Hawk asked mildly, not even knowing why he was bothering. What these people did or didn't do or have, he told himself, made no difference to him as long as they didn't interfere with his life.

"Reformed hair-trigger temper," Teri corrected, coming to her younger sister's defense. "Apparently," she added, looking at Hawk significantly, "there's hope for everyone."

Really time for him to go, Hawk thought. "As long as you don't raise the bar too high." He rose from the small table that barely accommodated the four of them. He looked at Teri. "Thanks for the drink. I'll see you tomorrow."

Before she could say anything further, he was on his way to the front door. With a sigh, Teri lifted her mug again.

"Talkative devil," Callie commented, watching Hawk disappear into the crowd.

"I'm sure that he'd tell you Teri makes up for it." Shaw grinned at his middle sister.

Callie downed the last of her own beer, setting the mug on the table. "Reminds me of Patrick before his epiphany." She rose. "Time for me to call it a day, too." She stretched a little like someone coming out of a confining space. "A long one."

Nodding, Teri got up, as well. Shaw was already on his feet. She wanted to ask her question before they left. She'd been waiting to get them alone, not wanting to have to hear Hawk make another comment about privacy. "Do either one of you have any idea what Dad might be dropping off at the criminal lab?"

Callie, looking mildly interested, hesitated as if waiting for a punch line. "No, why?"

"I bumped into him earlier today and he didn't say a word about it, but Mulrooney told me he saw Dad with Claude Wilkins. According to Mulrooney, Dad was giving him a spoon and a book."

"Maybe it was a gift," Shaw suggested.

That would have been her take on it, if Wilkins hadn't seemed so reticent to disclose any information. "When I asked Wilkins about it, he said he wasn't comfortable discussing the matter."

Callie looked unfazed. "If Dad wants us to know, he'll tell us. He's never kept secrets from us," she reminded her.

"Maybe it has to do with Mom." The thought had lingered on Teri's mind all afternoon and now the words came blurting out. The others looked at her. "You know how he gets."

Shaw exchanged looks with Callie. It was a gray area they talked about less and less. "All the more reason not to ask him for details. He needs to let go and he will in his own time. The rest of us have."

Had they? Teri wondered several minutes later as she walked to the far end of the open parking lot and her car. She knew they all said they had accepted what everyone felt was the inevitable, but in their hearts, had they? Had they really extinguished all hope that maybe, just maybe, against all odds, their mother was still out there?

Teri knew there were times, in the dead of night, when the loneliness would come creeping in like a deadly cancer and she'd wanted to cling to the belief that her mother would come home.

But then daylight would come, pushing away the somber thoughts, the unrealistic scenarios, and she would take up the rest of her life, knowing her mother was gone.

"Stop it, Teri," she upbraided herself sharply as she turned on the engine, "you've got a case to solve. Don't go thinking about things that have no solution." There was never going to be a final answer as to what became of their mother. The most likely scenario was one she didn't want to entertain. Her mother was gone. That was the bottom line and she had to make her peace with that. Again.

But then, she was always tilting at windmills, always taking up challenges that no one else wanted.

Like bringing Hawk out of his armored shell.

The evening hadn't exactly gone swimmingly, but he had come out. He had accompanied her to the Shannon, she reminded herself. That had been a first and she shouldn't be minimizing it.

One small step for Hawk, one giant leap for me.

With a smile, she pulled out of the space, her eyes glued to the rearview mirror, alert for any lit taillights. After several minutes, she was on the road, heading for home and rest.

Though she hated to admit it, she suddenly felt overwhelmingly tired and was secretly glad to be on her way home. As always, her stubbornness had caused her to overdo it. But they'd have to pry the admission from her cold, cold lips because she'd never readily own up to the fact that maybe her father was right and that she should have remained home an extra day.

When she saw the porch lights at her house, she sighed with relief.

The telephone rang at eight that evening, its shrill noise breaking into the silence that hovered around the house tonight. Andrew hadn't felt like turning on the TV or the radio. He was too afraid he might not hear the phone when it rang.

Before the first ring had died away, he had the receiver up and against his ear.

For all intents and purposes, he was alone here tonight. Teri had gone to bed after a light supper, for once listening to him about getting her rest. She'd looked ghastly pale this evening. It's what she got for being so stubborn.

For being his daughter, he'd thought, because he would have done exactly what she had and gotten back up on the horse that had thrown him. She was that determined to break a case, one that went beyond a single simple home invasion.

"Hello?" His own voice sounded a little breathless to his ear. But he'd been waiting for this call. Waiting for it even before he'd left the crime lab.

"Andy, it's Claude."

Andrew could feel his pulse accelerating. He dispensed with his customary cheerful chitchat. There was only one thought on his mind. One thought that had been there all afternoon, stilling his brain activity to such an extent that he had exchanged perhaps ten sentences with Teri from the time she came home to the time she had gone to her room.

Not since Rose had first disappeared had he felt such a high level of anticipation wrapped in dread. "Did they match?"

There was a long sigh on the other end of the line. Andrew braced himself for disappointment. "Had some trouble getting a clear print."

C'mon, c'mon, don't talk me to death, just tell me what I need to know. He knew how Wilkins worked. "But you did."

"I did. Finally."

Claude Wilkins was the best at what he did, none better. But the man was incredibly long-winded and given half an opportunity, could talk on for hours about virtually nothing. And this was far from nothing. This was his very future on the line.

"And?" Andrew urged, trying to curb his impatience and keep from snapping at the man he'd known for over thirty-five years.

"They match. Whose are they, Andy?"

He had refrained from telling the head technician his hopes on the matter. He knew what the others thought, how they felt. Pity was something he had no desire to encounter again. "They belong to someone I once knew."

"Long-lost friend?" Wilkins probed.

"Yeah." It was a safe enough answer, although she'd been more than a friend, more than a wife to him. Rose Gallagher Cavanaugh had been the other half of his soul, and he'd been incomplete ever since she'd disappeared. "Thanks, Claude, I owe you one."

He heard a soft chuckle on the other end of the time. "Prime rib dinner comes to mind."

Wilkins had wandered onto territory reserved for the other major love of his life after his family and police work. Cooking. "You got it. I'll be by for the spoon and book tomorrow." About to hang up, there was something in the other man's tone that stopped him.

"Oh, I think you should know. Teri came by this afternoon and asked if you'd left something for me to examine."

"What did you say?"

Wilkins was glib and open. "That I wasn't comfortable talking about it. Not a hell of a whole lot I could have told her, anyway, Andy," he pointed out.

"You never said who you thought the prints belonged to."

"No," Andrew said with finality, terminating this part of the conversation. "I didn't. Dinner sometime next week all right with you?"

If he felt he was being dealt with abruptly, Wilkins gave no indication of it in his voice. "You're on. Just call and tell me when. I'll bring my appetite."

Saying something that passed for appropriate, Andrew hung up. He'd barely heard Wilkins. Even thoughts of possibly being discovered by his daughter before he was ready to share this with them slipped into the far recesses of his mind.

He'd found her.

After all this time, he'd found her. He'd known it all along. Known that she was alive.

Tears gathered in his eyes.

Tears of joy.

And tears of sorrow, for everything Rose had missed over these last fifteen years.

"So, was it good for you?" Teri asked cheerfully as she walked into the squad room.

Her question was directed toward Hawk who was just hanging up the phone. His desk, including the keyboard he rarely used, was completely covered with notes he'd been poring over since early this morning. He looked up now and sent a dark look his partner's way.

"It was good for me," she told Hawk when he made no response.

When she'd woken up this morning, she'd felt as if her world was completely filled with sunshine. Never a sluggish riser, the way her younger sister, Rayne, was, this was still an unusual high even for her and she had nothing to pin it on—except perhaps that she had finally gotten Hawk to come to the Shannon. Success, no matter how minor, always felt good.

The look Hawk gave her was that much darker because her question had aroused a scenario in his head that had no place being there.

"Hey, you two talking about what I think you're talking about?" Mulrooney asked, lowering his voice even as his eyes darted from her to Hawk and then back again.

"Number one," Hawk began tersely, "I'm not talking, she is so there is no 'two' here. And number two, God only knows what Cavanaugh is babbling about this time."

"I'm in too good a mood to let your grumpiness affect me," she informed Hawk. Coming up behind Hawk's chair, she placed her hands on his shoulders as if he were a budding protégé she was sponsoring for an exclusive club. "You weren't there, Dan, but Hawk here finally made it to the Shannon last night." She beamed down at him. God, but he had thick, black hair. The kind that tempted a woman to run her fingers through it. She leaned her face down to be level with his. "So, the next office barbecue, your place?"

Hawk purposely turned around in his chair, breaking the connection. Funny, he could almost still feel her hands on his shoulders. "If I'd known you'd act this crazy, I would have never said yes. What the hell's gotten into you this morning?"

"I don't know," she said honestly. "Maybe I'm just glad to be alive."

Mulrooney laughed shortly. "Yeah," he agreed. "The alternative really stinks."

"All depends on your take on this life and the afterlife," his partner, Tom Kassidy, a man half his girth and almost half Mulrooney's height, piped up as he joined the forum.

Teri looked at her partner. "How about it, Hawk? Do you believe in an afterlife?"

Hawk looked at her pointedly. "Wouldn't know about that." He wrote something down on his small, worn pad before sticking it back into the pocket of his jacket. "I'm pretty sure about hell on earth, though."

Mulrooney laughed as he crossed to the doorway. It was time to scrounge up his morning snack from the vending machine. "He's got you there, Cavanaugh."

Actually, Teri thought, looking at Hawk, the man had her in a lot of ways she didn't have time to dwell on right now.

"So," she began, just as cheerfully as she had before, settling in behind her desk, "we find anything new on the home invasions?" As far as she knew, Hawk didn't get any personal calls. He hadn't in the nine months they'd been together. Which meant that the call he'd just finished had to have something to do with work. With their case if they were lucky.

Hawk rose to his feet. "I'm going to check out something."

She stood in an instant, picking up the small shoulder purse she hadn't had time to put away yet. "Okay."

"Alone." The look he tossed over his shoulder was meant to glue her feet in place.

It didn't.

"Hey, we're partners, remember?" She fell into step beside him. "Where you go, I go—unless it's the men's room."

He paused, debating. He really did prefer doing things alone, especially when it came to seeing his contacts. But there was no reason he could give her that would make her stay in the office. "You can come, as long as you leave the sunshiny attitude behind."

She saluted, earning herself a deeper frown. "I'll do my best."

Without saying another word, he led the way out of the office. He had a feeling that her best was going to fall woefully short of his expectations.

Chapter Seven

The alleyway between the two crumbling buildings was enshrouded in darkness despite the sunshine that existed on the street just beyond the perimeter. It was as if nothing bright could be allowed to enter here—no sunshine, no hope.

The air was foul, filled with the smell of decay and rotting garbage the city had neglected to pick up. Pickup was sporadic.

Following behind Hawk, Teri glanced over her shoulder toward the curb where he'd left the car parked, wondering if they would find it in one piece when they were finished here.

Teri nearly tripped over what she thought was a mound of garbage, catching her balance just in time.

The mound moved, drawing into itself. She sucked in her breath. Two eyes stared out at her from somewhere within the pile of filthy rags, then closed again into slits before disappearing altogether.

Adrenaline doing double time, she felt for her weapon as she hurried to keep up pace with Hawk. The phone call he'd received earlier had brought them here, to this unlikely place where people existed in the moment, hoping the next would not be as bad as the one they were in. He'd been typically uncommunicative, only saying that the call was from someone about a tip regarding the home invasions. She assumed it had to be one of his snitches.

She scanned the area. Beyond the person beneath the rags, there didn't seem to be anyone else around. Just who was he meeting? "Is this where you hang out when you're not working?"

He glanced in her direction, wishing she was back in the office. He was at home here; she wasn't. "Nobody asked you to come."

And the friendliness continues. "You're my partner," she emphasized. "I'm supposed to have your back, remember?"

He led the way to where four sagging buildings in various degrees of disrepair stood with their backs to one another, like feuding members of a family who had long since forgotten why they had gotten angry in the first place.

"Nothing'll happen to me here."

Hawk said the words with resignation rather than

confidence. "Now who's being a superhero?" she asked.

His answer made the smile fade from her lips. "I grew up here." Pointing off toward what appeared to be an abandoned apartment building that had been dark and dreary long before it began to crumble, he said, "There. Third floor. In the back." His voice was completely devoid of any emotion.

She stared at the building that had only rats and the homeless for its tenants now. Sympathy flooded through her. "My God," she whispered.

Picking his way farther into the shadows, Hawk spared her a hint of a cynical smile. "No. He never came calling." Memories crowded into his head. Horrible memories he pushed back. "These were the people even He gave up on."

They stopped by the next alley. She stared at Hawk, not knowing what to say. The last thing he wanted was pity and it wasn't really pity she was feeling. Just a tremendous desire to comfort, to somehow erase that period of time from his mind. To help him pretend it never happened.

But before she could find the words she needed, she saw someone coming. Teri tensed as a dirty-looking man in even dirtier fatigues walked toward them.

Toward Hawk.

Seemingly oblivious to the weather, the man wasn't wearing a jacket. He was scratching at his arm as if trying to systematically tear away the flesh and get clear down to the bone.

This was who they'd come to meet.

The thought telegraphed itself through her brain. She looked at Hawk for a sign of recognition.

To her surprise, Hawk smiled. "Hey, Jocko, how's it going?"

The man shrugged paper-thin shoulders that echoed within a shirt that might have fit him once, but was now at least two sizes too large.

"Complaining ain't gonna do me no good." And then his red-rimmed, bloodshot eyes brightened. "But you look good, man."

"Thanks." Hawk hated seeing the man this way, hated it because he knew what Jack Armstrong had once looked like, had once been. But drugs and alcohol had long since destroyed that man, leaving behind only a shell that went through the motions of living. "You have something for me?" He saw Jocko's eyes dart toward his partner. "She's okay."

"She's more than okay, Jackie." The man smiled and Teri saw that he had more spaces than teeth in his mouth. "She's fine." Jocko drew out the last word as if he was savoring it. As if he was remembering another time when women mattered in his life. "You got a name, pretty lady?"

There was something about the derelict that told her she had nothing to fear, even if Hawk hadn't been standing next to her. Even if she hadn't a loaded weapon at her disposal. She smiled at him. "Teri."

"Teri," the man repeated as if he was in love with the name.

Any second now Jocko's thoughts would wander, taking with it what he needed to know. He'd seen it happen before. Hawk laid a hand on the man's shoulder, hating the feel of his bones as they met his touch. "Jocko, what do you have to tell me?"

Jocko ran his tongue along his lips. His eyes looked a little crazed as he drew back into his life, retreating from the momentary respite he'd sought. He struggled to think.

"I do a little 'donation gathering' around Bancroft Avenue, you know, where all those restaurants are. Kind of upscale for me, but you know, man's gotta try." He shrugged. "One of the chefs there behind Angelino's, sometimes he gives me a little something to tide me over."

"Food?" Teri asked only to have Hawk give her a silencing look.

"For the soul, pretty lady. Food for the soul," Jocko told her with a wide grin. Hawk tapped his shoulder and he returned to his narrative. "I heard these two guys talking last night. They didn't see me there."

"What two guys?" Hawk pressed.

But his thoughts already appeared to be fading. Jocko frowned as he tried to think. "I dunno. Guys in uniforms."

"Soldiers?" Teri suggested.

"No." Jocko looked down at the fatigues he was

wearing, then shook his head. "Not like this. Just something that made them look alike." He looked up at Hawk. "One guy was talking about maybe laying low for a while now that those two guys were caught for the home invasion. The other guy said that once the guys were out, they could maybe make a big score, then move on somewhere else, like before." He licked his lips again. "Did I do good, calling you?" And then he grinned again. "A cop. Who'd've thought it?"

Hawk stared into the other man's eyes, willing him to focus, to pull up this one incident from his jumbled brain. "Think, Jocko. What kind of uniforms?"

Jocko sighed, shaking his head helplessly.

"Were they waiters?" Hawk asked. "Chefs, interns?" To each question, Jocko just continued shaking his head. Exasperated, Hawk looked at Teri. "Help me out here. Who else wears uniforms?"

"Policemen, firemen—" The list was endless and they were wasting time. Maybe there was another way. "Can you describe the uniforms, Jocko?"

Jocko looked down at his worn, cracked boots. "I was a little out of it," he confessed sheepishly. But because there were two sets of eyes looking at him, he scrubbed his face with his hands, searching for a piece of something more to offer. And then he brightened. "Red. They had on red jackets."

She looked at Hawk. Who wore red jackets? "Doormen?" she guessed out loud. "No, wait. Valets." That seemed more likely. There were a score of valet services up and down Bancroft in the area Jocko had described. "Were they valets?"

Jocko only looked at her blankly, as if he didn't understand the word she'd used. And then he turned toward Hawk. The expression on his face testified that his attention span was almost gone.

"Did I do good?"

Hawk smiled at the man. Teri could swear there was even warmth in his voice.

"You did good, Jocko." Digging into his pocket, Hawk took out two hundred-dollar bills. He pressed them into the filthy palm. "Here. Clean up a little."

Gleefully, Jocko looked at his windfall, then carefully placed the bounty into the one pocket that wasn't torn clean through.

"Absolutely. That's what I'm going to do. Clean up. Soon as you go, I'm going to head off to the mission and clean up. Start a new life—you'll see. Thanks, Jackie. You would have done them proud." Teri watched as the babbling man grew misty. "You take care now."

He scrambled away before either one of them could say anything more.

Teri turned away from where they'd met the man and fell into step beside Hawk as they made their way out of the alley. "He's going to use the money to buy alcohol, you know that."

Yes, he knew that. But the battle for Jack Armstrong and his soul had long since been lost.

"Yeah, maybe." His voice was steely again. Removed. "More than likely, he'll use it to score some drugs."

Emerging out into the sun again, Teri saw that their ride was still there, untouched. It seemed almost incredible, given their location. "You gave him money to buy drugs?"

"No, I gave him money for information. What he does with it is his business." He rounded the hood and got in on the driver's side. His emotions, though blanketed, were on a dangerous edge. "Don't get on your high horse with me, Cavanaugh."

He started up the car and peeled away from the curb, just as he had once peeled away from this neighborhood, gasping for air and something clean to look forward to. He hadn't quite found it yet and probably never would, but he could live with that. Growing up here had taught him he could live with a lot of things, as long as it meant continuing for another day.

He didn't bother looking at her. His thoughts were still with Jocko. It had been over six months since he'd last seen the man. Each time, he looked a little worse.

"Until you've lived on these streets, don't preach."

"I'm not preaching," she insisted, taking offense. "I just thought that helping Jocko really get clean instead of just tossing money at him—"

She saw him set his jaw hard. "Doctor at the free clinic gave him maybe six months. He wants to spend it in oblivion, that's his choice."

How terrible, she thought, to have nothing to look

forward to except the numbing oblivion that came from drugs. "Where do you *know* this man from?"

He laughed shortly, ready to dismiss the question. Hawk had no idea what made him answer it. "He was my father's best friend. Jack Armstrong. My mother named me after him. Jocko kept my father from branding me once. I owe him."

Teri felt as if someone had just punched her in the stomach. "Branding you? My God, Hawk, that's awful."

Hawk blew out a breath. The incident had occurred over twenty years ago, yet it hovered around his brain as if it had been last week.

"No, awful would have been if my father had succeeded. Jocko was a lot more together then than he is now." Shaking his head, he took a corner. The neighborhoods slowly got better, the despair receding into the background. "He's a pretty decent guy who just never had enough willpower to walk away from what was keeping him down."

"What gave you willpower?" she asked quietly.

Hawk looked at her sharply. He knew what she was asking him. She wanted to know what had kept him from sinking into the mire he'd found himself standing in.

"I didn't want to be like my old man. Ever." How did she do that—get him to talk when he had no intentions of talking? "Look, this isn't something I want to discuss, okay?"

He'd opened a door and she didn't want it shutting again. "You brought up the subject."

She was nitpicking, he thought angrily. "You asked me where I knew him from."

She wanted to set the record straight. He'd been the one to start the ball rolling, not her. "But you said you grew up around here." Shifting in her seat, she turned toward him. "Hawk, I don't want to pry—"

He snorted. "Well, then you're doing a damn poor job of it."

"But sometimes, when you keep something like that inside of you for too long, it can make you break apart."

He rolled his eyes as he eased through a green light. "Any shrinks in your family?"

"No."

Hawk turned in her direction before switching lanes. "You trying out for the position?"

"No, I'm trying out for the position of partner."

The radio crackled, but no message followed. Just his luck. "'Case you haven't noticed, you already are my partner."

It took more than a coupling to accomplish that. She wanted what everyone in her family had. What she'd grown up believing in. Partners knew each other inside and out. They were there for one another, come hell or high water, no matter what. That didn't begin to describe what existed between them.

"We sit next to each other in the car every day, and in the office, but you don't share."

He scowled at her. Why hadn't he gone with his first instinct and just disappeared on his way to the men's room? She didn't need to come with him. "You never stop talking. Nobody else can get in a word edgewise."

She was one step ahead of him. "You wouldn't start talking to me if I did stop."

He laughed, savoring the thought. "No, but the peace would be nice."

"Hawk, partners share things."

Maybe in her world, but not in his. "I didn't even know one of my partners had kids until they showed up at his retirement party. We talked about work, which we were getting paid for." He looked at her, his point clear. "Nobody was paying us to be best friends."

She seized on the word. "Have you even ever had a best friend?"

"No, but I've had an urge to wrap my fingers around a throat as white as snow." His patience snapped. He shouldn't have to have this discussion if he didn't want to. What was it about this woman that brought his emotions to a full boil? "Damn it, Cavanaugh, I don't need a friend, a father confessor or a shrink."

She braced herself as he flew through the light. She could always tell when she got to him. He drove faster. "You work it right, a friend can be all of that."

He bit back the curse that rose to his lips. It wouldn't solve anything and she'd probably come up with a bar of soap to use on his mouth. "You just don't stop, do you?"

When he looked in her direction again, she moved her head from side to side. "Nope."

This time, he did mutter an oath, albeit a mild one. "You're like that kid's story about the train—"

It took her a minute to realize what he was referring to. "You mean *The Little Engine That Could*?"

"Yeah, that one." He turned right on the corner. "Pushing and shoving, being a damn pain in the butt, until you make it up over that hill."

"Who read you a story?"

Her question, asked so softly, caught him off guard. He shrugged. "They read it in school once." Why was he even telling her that? Why was he telling her anything? Every time he tried to clam up, she was at him with a crowbar and he didn't even realize it. "Cavanaugh, I don't pry into your life—"

She spread her hands innocently. "Pry away, it's an open book."

He didn't want to pry. The less he knew about her, the better. She was already haunting his thoughts far more than he was happy about. To know anything more about her might increase her occupancy time. "That's your problem, not mine."

It never bothered her to be too open. She had no secrets, other than a deep fear of commitment, of being hurt. But that certainly wasn't in play here. "Okay, but someday, you're going to need a friend. And when you do, I'm here."

That sounded more like a threat to him than a promise. He sighed. "Until then, could you make like a silent partner?"

"Sorry."

And then he laughed. "Didn't think so. I guess that sort of thing comes under the heading of miracles."

"Looks to me as if you've already had a slice of that."

Hawk pulled up into the parking lot. "How do you figure?"

He expected Cavanaugh to say something about his having her as a partner, but instead, she said, "You got out of your old neighborhood in one piece."

Almost one piece, he thought. But the mean streets had left their mark on him and it wasn't the kind of mark that anything could ever wash away.

He kept that to himself.

Andrew's body felt stiff as he brought his car to a halt in the parking lot. It was the tension rather than his years that was taking its toll on him. He'd felt it ever since he'd gotten into his car earlier.

Turning off the ignition, he sat behind the wheel for a moment. Gathering his thoughts. Gathering his courage. Beside him on the passenger seat was their family album and Rose's copy of *Gone with the Wind*. Evidence to prove his case.

He wavered, debating turning back. Debating bringing one of his kids with him. Callie was the convincing one and he wished she was here with him now.

Damn it, a man shouldn't be afraid to see his own wife.

But he was. Afraid of rejection. Afraid that what would happen here would destroy the fabric of the life he'd woven together these past fifteen years for himself and the kids. A life that was still missing one thing.

Rose.

He'd wanted to call the family together and tell them about the fingerprints. That he'd been right all along. That their mother was alive. Twice he'd even picked up the phone to call Brian and tell him about it. But each time he'd hung up before the call went through.

This was something he needed to face himself, to do himself. The others could know later.

Rayne had been the one who'd seen Rose first. On her way to Bainbridge-by-the-sea on a case, his youngest had stopped at the diner and seen the woman who called herself Claire. The resemblance was so strong, Rayne had been struck by it immediately. She'd come home to tell him about it, about possibly seeing her mother.

But she hadn't asked him if he'd gone to see for himself, hadn't asked him anything at all. It was as if she'd uttered a silent plea that until he was certain, she didn't want to hear anything.

He knew how that could be.

And he was certain.

But it wasn't enough. She had to come back with him. Rose had to come back home.

So here he was, sitting in the diner's parking lot, steeling himself off so that he could convince her by using photographs of their life together, photographs of the children they'd had, both looking the way they'd looked when she'd disappeared and the way they looked now.

He needed to know where she'd been for fifteen years and why she didn't remember him.

The pit of his stomach felt as if it were harboring a cannonball. Praying, he got out, the album and novel under his arm.

When he walked in, the diner was empty except for the sunlight that filled it.

Rose wasn't anywhere to be seen.

For a moment, his heart froze. Had she disappeared again? Had he imagined it all? Imagined her? No, the fingerprints were real. And Rayne had seen her, too. It wasn't just him.

Over in the corner, the cashier looked up from the magazine she was reading. "Can I help you?"

He crossed to her, hoping she could. "Excuse me, is Rose—I mean, is Claire around?"

The heavyset woman beamed. "No, she's off today. Just me and my husband here today, I'm afraid." She began to rise from her perch. "Everybody always asks for Claire. That smile of hers brings in a lot of business. What'll you have?"

"Do you know where I can find her?" He saw a wary look come into the woman's brown eyes. He lowered his eyes to her name tag. "Lucy."

She shook her head. Her smile was sympathetic. "I'm sorry, but I can't—"

She probably thought he was some kind of stalker, Andrew guessed. "It's really important I find her. I need to talk to her." Before she could turn him down or call her husband out, Andrew opened the album and placed it on the counter between them. He pointed to the photograph of a young Rose surrounded by their children. He was standing next to her. "I'm her husband. I've been trying to find her for fifteen years."

Lucy's mouth fell open.

Half an hour later, he was standing before the door of a garden apartment, feeling as if his very life were on the line. He'd chased down dark alleys after perps with less fear than he was feeling now.

He'd told his story to Lucy and the woman had been deeply moved. She'd pored over the photographs in the album, saying that she'd known all along that had to be more to Claire's life than what the woman had told her. Claire had turned up at their diner fifteen years ago, looking for work, having no place to stay. She'd seemed overwrought and nervous. Lucy told him that she and her husband had put Claire up for a few weeks and when she'd gotten together enough money, she moved into a place of her own.

No one, Lucy said, could have asked for a better, more tireless worker. Lucy loved her like a daughter.

At the end of her story, she'd given him Claire's address.

The door opened on his first knock.

His Rose was in the doorway, her hand on the doorjamb, her body blocking any access.

"Lucy called me," she explained. She looked at him hesitantly. "You're the man who came into the diner the other day."

They had history—years together—not just a few moments over opposite sides of a cup of coffee, he wanted to shout. Instead he whispered, "Don't you know me?"

"You're the man who came in the other day," she repeated, as if clinging to that piece of information.

"Rose," he began, reaching out to her.

She pulled back, but still blocked his way into her apartment. It was obvious she didn't want him to come in. "My name is Claire," she insisted. "I don't know a Rose. Please go away."

He'd waited too long to be sent away like this. "Rose, I'm your husband. I've been looking for you for fifteen years."

She swallowed, uncertain. Afraid. That old, haunting feeling was coming back. The one that stole into her dreams, making them nightmares. She tried vainly to block it. "If you were my husband, something inside of me would know you. I'm sorry, but—"

Desperate, Andrew opened the album and held it up in front of him. "Look, this is you holding Callie. She's our first daughter. And here's Shaw, that's our oldest boy. And here—"

Shutting her eyes, she shook her head. "I don't remember. I don't remember," she repeated more loudly. "I don't know who any of these people are." He was frightening her now. Images were flashing through her brain like sections of an electrical storm. It'd been like that when she'd first come to. Just before that man had picked her up on the side of the road. The one who'd tried to force himself on her. She'd thrown herself from the car just in time. The past frightened her. She'd given up trying to remember it. "I'm sorry you can't find your wife, but she's not me."

"What were your parents' names?"

She stared at him. "I don't know."

"Amy and Bill Gallagher," he told her. Her parents were dead now. They'd died thinking their only child had drowned. Andrew fired another question at her, trying desperately to shake her, to get to her. "Where were you born?"

"I don't know!" Her voice cracked.

He wanted to take her into his arms, to hold her, but he knew that would only frighten her more. "Aurora, California. The same place where we lived. Where the kids and I still live. Aurora," he repeated.

There was no flicker of recognition in her eyes. She began to shut the door. He spoke more rapidly. "Your name is Rose Gallagher Cavanaugh. We met in elementary school and got married before I graduated from the police academy. All of them followed, you know—the kids, they all work at the police department. And they miss you very, very much."

She didn't want this, didn't want to make the nightmares come back. He had to leave. "Look, I'm sorry you came up all this way for nothing, but I'm not the woman you're looking for."

He put his hand up as she started to close the door. "I matched your prints." She stopped to look at him, confusion on her face. Andrew fished a spoon out of his pocket and held it up. "I took this from the diner and matched the prints on it to the ones that were on your favorite book." Handing the spoon to her, he showed her the novel. "*Gone with the Wind.* Remember?" He peered at her face, but there was nothing to indicate that he'd broken through. "You used to like to read it every night. I told you I felt like I was competing with Rhett Butler."

When he offered her the book, she pushed it away. "No, I don't remember. I don't remember anything. Please leave me alone." This time, she managed to close the door on him.

Andrew stood staring at the door for several moments, waiting for her to open it again. Waiting for her to come out and tell him that she'd changed her mind, that she'd hear him out.

She didn't.

He took out a card from his pocket, one of the old ones that had his number at the precinct on it. He'd crossed out the number and written in his home number instead. Andrew stuck it inside the book beside the dedication.

Bending down, he placed Rose's book down on the doormat that cheerfully proclaimed Welcome and then walked away.

Chapter Eight

She was getting to him.

Hawk stopped looking over the files spread across his desk, stopped pretending he was reading them. Because he wasn't. He'd been stuck on the same damn sentence for over ten minutes now. Stuck on it and it still hadn't registered.

He'd never thought it could be possible. It had taken nine months, but she *was* getting to him. Giving no warning, sounding no alarms. Odorless, tasteless, invisible, like carbon monoxide, Teri Cavanaugh had somehow managed to slip into his system.

He would have said that it had all started when his partner had been looped on painkillers and had kissed him in the car, but that, if anything, had just been the trigger. The process had begun a lot earlier than that, although for the life of him, Hawk couldn't pinpoint exactly when.

He was attracted to her.

Attracted physically and emotionally, although he would have been the last person to think the latter was possible for him. But if not, why else would he have told her about Jocko? Why else would he have allowed her even a glimpse into the life he'd once led? Why else had he opened up the smallest bit to her, he who conducted himself with the gregariousness of a clam?

There was no other explanation. Thoughts of Teri popped into his mind at random times, completely unrelated to whatever he was thinking.

Because she'd gotten to him.

Gotten to him with her nails-on-chalkboard-grating cheerfulness and her over-the-top optimism.

Cavanaugh was a cop, for Pete's sake. The daughter of a head cop. She knew about the kinds of people who had once populated his own world exclusively. And her mother had died when she was still a kid. How the hell could Cavanaugh maintain her upbeat attitude against those kinds of things?

And yet she did. And because she did, because she seemed to care about everything and everyone, she'd somehow managed to get to him. To burrow her way under his skin and take up residence.

He didn't want to be gotten.

He wanted to continue just as he was, being a dedicated detective working the cases he was assigned. He didn't need a social life, didn't need anything at all beyond that. Just work, just the feeling that somehow, some way, he was making the slightest bit of difference by tilting the balance between good and evil to the plus side just a fraction.

That was all he needed.

But now, with this—this woman buzzing around in his life like an annoying hummingbird that wouldn't fly away, he needed more.

Wanted more.

Wanted her, he realized with a shock that coursed through his body.

She felt Hawk's gaze before she ever looked up from her desk. When she did, she couldn't read his expression.

So what else was new?

She straightened, pushing her shoulders back just a little. Like a prisoner standing against a wall, facing execution without knowing the crime.

"What, am I wearing my lunch?" She ran a thumb quickly along either side of her mouth even as she asked. Lunch had been a sandwich grabbed from a popular fast-food restaurant.

Hawk shook his head. "Just thinking."

"You looked as if you were shooting darts in my direction. Anything I did? Lately," she qualified before he could launch into a list of her shortcomings. Her sins in his eyes were many, at the top of which was probably breathing.

"Nothing you can help," he muttered, looking back at his notes.

Okay, what did that mean? And why, in the middle of a growing investigation that was bringing more and more home invasions with similar M.O.'s to the fore, did she suddenly feel as if goose bumps were forming up and down, all along her arms? Goose bumps were connected to being cold, to fear and to feelings.

The last thing in the world she needed was to have feelings for her partner. That way always led to trouble, and when that partner was a monosyllabic, scowling man who'd rather cut her dead than talk to her, trouble suddenly took on a whole new meaning.

If he knew, if he suspected the growing attraction she felt for him, Hawkins would be out looking for a new partner before she could count to one.

She didn't want that. She was finally breaking him in to where he was, if not comfortably predictable—because with Hawk there was no comfort zone—at least to where they had some kind of a moderate rhythm worked out. She didn't want to lose it.

Get your mind back on your work. At least that's safe territory.

Leaning back in her chair, Teri looked at the new case files that had recently been added to the pile on her desk. These involved people who had reported home invasions as far back as three years ago. She'd been looking them over since she'd come in this morning, and had found only one pattern. The income and lifestyle of the people had been so diverse and they'd been so scattered across the city that the M.O. hadn't really stood out until someone went looking for it.

Not one of them showed any signs of forced entry.

Tossing aside the pen she'd been chewing on, she voiced out loud the thought that suddenly came to her. "What if they didn't start out doing home invasions?"

Hawk raised his eyes in her direction again. "What do you mean?"

She pulled her chair in closer, drawing nearer to Hawk. "What if they started out doing simple burglaries, you know, when the people weren't home." The more the idea gelled, the more excited she became. This could open up doors. "Maybe they graduated first to home invasions, for the kicks of pulling it off in front of an audience, then went on to culling their quarry so that they only hit the ones they knew for certain were well-off—the ones who drove the most expensive cars," she concluded, pulling in the piece of information they were still trying to follow up on, that of the lead Jocko had given them. "With whatever nest egg they'd accumulated to fall back on, they could afford to be a little discriminating. Hit the right place, it's worth hitting three other lesser affluent ones." She beamed at him, finished. "We clear this up, we could be clearing a whole rash of burglaries."

He supposed the idea had merit, at least enough to

check out the possibilities. "How far back you want to go?"

She thought a second. The ones on her desk and his already went back three years. "Five years should give us a good foothold."

Back from lunch, a container of black coffee in one hand and a package of cupcakes in the other, Mulrooney walked in on the tail end of her statement. He looked from Hawk to Teri. "You want to investigate five years' worth of burglaries?" The question was punctuated with a groan.

"Just the ones without signs of forced entry," she qualified.

Kassidy was bringing up his partner's rear and stopped cold. "And then what?"

Teri said the only thing that followed logically. "And then we talk to the victims and find out if they'd ever gone to a restaurant along Bancroft Avenue before the burglary took place."

Hawk had another take on the matter. "Too exclusive." She looked at him quizzically. "Spread the net wider. See if any of the victims ever used a valet service of any kind, anyplace." Valet services were not restricted to just restaurants. "We get a pattern, we can start focusing on specific valet services."

Mulrooney's eyes narrowed. "You think someone at a valet service is behind the home invasions? Why?"

"Got a tip," Hawk told him. "The idea bears checking out." He looked at the two men across from him. He could see that neither one of them thought very highly of the speculation. "Hey, until something better comes along, we go with this."

"You're the primary." Mulrooney sighed. Then his small eyes darted toward Teri accusingly. He'd picked up enough to know who was behind the idea. "Think this is a waste of time," he muttered, trudging off to his desk. Kassidy followed behind him, shaking his head the way he always did whenever there was extra work to do.

"Nice work," Hawk said almost under his breath after the other two detectives had gone to their desks.

Teri raised her eyes. "Excuse me?" She tilted her head, as if to hear better. "Were you talking to yourself, or was that a general comment?"

"Neither." Hawk sighed. He should have never said anything in the first place. "It was intended for you."

She smiled in mild triumph. "Might be nice to hear it said a little louder."

"Don't push it, Cavanaugh. It was a good idea. That doesn't mean it's going to get us anywhere."

"I think it is." Teri leaned her head on her up-turned palm. "Care to make a small wager?"

His scowl deepened. "I don't bet."

The way her mouth curved smugly got under his skin. "Afraid you'll lose?"

He surprised himself by asking, "What kind of a wager?"

Mentally Teri rubbed her hands together. "If I win, you come to breakfast at my house."

He thought of the Shannon. "Is this another one of your attempts at trying to 'socialize' me?"

It was, but she wasn't about to admit it. "No, it's just letting my dad finally meet my partner." He'd met all her siblings' partners and he'd once been partnered with the man who'd preceded Hawk. But since Hawk never attended any group functions, her father had never met him. "Besides, he makes a mean Belgian waffle."

"The chief cooks?"

What planet had he been living on? Everyone knew her father was every bit as good with a spatula as he was with a service revolver. But then, this was Hawk, who rarely listened to anything that went on in the precinct unless it was work related.

"Like a dream," she declared. "He put himself through school and the academy by working as a chef. My father could cook rings around my mother—when he had the chance. Most of the time, he didn't. Not until she…" Her voice trailed off. The next moment, she'd regrouped. "So, is it a bet?"

To her surprise, there was mild interest in his eyes. "What do I get if I win?"

His question caught her unprepared. "Huh? I really hadn't thought about you winning."

He laughed, shaking his head. Whatever else she was, he'd developed a healthy respect for her instincts when it came to the cases they worked. It hadn't come easily. At first glance, she looked like the classic bubble-headed blonde. Having her talk a mile a minute didn't exactly dispel the impression. But she'd worked hard and eventually, he'd changed his mind. The lady was sharp. "You're that sure about this?"

"I'm that sure."

Hawk blew out a breath, taking a momentary respite before trying to tackle his work again. "Must be nice." He had never been that sure of anything, other than himself and that he was meant to lead a solitary life. That was why having her around, rattling his cage, shaking up the foundations that he'd been so certain had been set in stone but were now quivering like Jell-O, was so damn unsettling. The last thing he was certain about—he wasn't anymore.

"Okay," Hawk finally said. "If you're wrong, you stop talking in the car for a month."

Her mouth dropped open. Did he hate the sound of her voice that much? "What?"

"You stop talking for a month when you're in the car."

She didn't know whether to tell him off, or laugh it off. "So I'm just supposed to sit there and not say anything?"

There was a flash of temper in her eyes. It intrigued him. "Right."

"What if you ask me a question?"

"I won't," he told her mildly. From somewhere deep inside, a smile was building, but he kept it from his lips.

Like a dog trying to pull a bone out of the ground, she wouldn't give up. "But if you do."

"Then you can talk." Hawk peered at her face, finding himself amused and enjoying this despite himself. "Not so convinced you're right anymore, are you?"

"Yes—" she drew herself up with a toss of her head "—I am. Okay, you're on. This leads us to a dead end I won't talk in the squad car."

"For a month," he reminded her.

She rolled her eyes. He could take things too far with the best of them, she thought. "For a month— unless you ask me to."

This time, he actually grinned. "I wouldn't hold my breath over that."

By the end of the day, through the combined efforts of the small task force the captain had allowed Hawk and Teri to pull together, they had come up with a total of thirty-six robberies and home invasions that had taken place in the last five years, all showing no signs of forced entry.

In the most recent cases, there were notations that several witnesses, including one victim, had actually seen the home invaders using a key to open the front door and get into the house.

Mulrooney tossed the last file he'd been reviewing on his desk. The contents spilled out, touching a pile of empty cellophane wrappers. He paused a moment before scooping up the papers and pushing them back between the manila file.

"How come nobody ever made the connection before?" he marveled.

The answer to that was simple. "Because they weren't looking for it," Teri told him. "And because it was just one of a thousand other pieces of information that was accumulated putting the cases together. Tomorrow, we start calling on these good people to find out if they'd ever used a valet service of any kind." Realizing that she'd usurped him again, she turned her chair toward Hawk. "Okay by you, fearless leader?"

He was surprised that she even bother to pretend to check with him. Cavanaugh was one of those women who just naturally took over. Another thing he had to be on the alert for. That she didn't just manage to naturally take over everything, him included.

"Sounds like a plan," he agreed. He should be irritated, he thought. Not that being a leader had ever mattered to him, but she was trying to make a run for the finish line and that was supposed to annoy him more than it did.

What the hell was going on here? he questioned himself again. As before, there was no real answer.

She slanted a look in his direction the moment the others were gone. "So, what's your favorite breakfast food?"

Hawk didn't bother looking up. "I don't eat breakfast."

He would once he attended one of her father's massive breakfasts. There was no food shortage here. Andrew Cavanaugh cooked as if he was trying to feed an army. "That'll change."

Okay, maybe he was getting tired of Cavanaugh taking over at that. "Since when did someone make you king of the world?"

"No king," she replied, giving him her most innocent face. "I just believe in honoring your debts, that's all."

"Very noble, but this isn't a debt yet. It's not over by a long shot."

She thumped the files. "You have to admit this is too much of a coincidence."

Ordinarily, he'd agree. But not when she was so damn cocksure of herself. It pushed him to the other side of the fence. "It still could be. People get careless, they leave their doors and windows unlocked. Could just be a matter of burglars seizing an opportunity."

"And could be more," she insisted quietly.

"Yeah," he allowed, getting back to work, not wanting to look in her direction any longer, not until he got himself back in the right gear. Right now, he was having all sorts of thoughts that were interfering with his work. "It could be more."

"Well, I'm going cross-eyed," Mulrooney announced to no one in particular as he tossed down a file. He rose to his feet. "Time to call it a day and head on home to the light of my life." The last phrase was uttered with more than a little sarcasm.

Teri looked in his direction. Mulrooney had been married to the same woman for over thirty years. The woman, in her opinion, deserved a medal for valor over and above the call of duty. "You're lucky Charlotte doesn't throw you out."

He pretended to take umbrage. "Hey, where she's going to find a better catch than me?"

"She's probably checking eBay right now," Kassidy cracked, powering down his computer. He pulled his things together, following his partner's lead.

Mulrooney laughed, but Teri noted that he tossed out the half-eaten candy bar he'd just brought back from the vending machine. The man's shadow could definitely use some toning down.

"You should talk." Mulrooney jeered at Kassidy as the two walked toward the door. "I don't know why your wife hasn't left you by now."

Kassidy laughed off the idea. "Haven't you heard? Us thin guys make great lovers."

"In your dreams," Mulrooney told him as they walked out of the office.

"No, in his wife's," Teri called out after the departing men.

Sitting back in her chair, Teri looked around. The office was almost chillingly quiet. For the first time today, she became aware of the hum of the fluorescent bulb just above her desk. That meant it was going to give up the ghost soon. Maybe she should, too. At least for tonight. Everyone else had already left for the day.

Except for Hawk.

He'd been here when she came in, early for once. And, from the looks of it, he would be here after she left.

She studied his profile for a moment. What went through his mind, she wondered. When he was alone, what did he think of?

"Do you ever wonder what it's like?" Teri finally asked.

More conversation. Resigned, Hawk raised his eyes to look at her. "What what's like?"

"Having someone to come home to." Was he lonely, she wondered. She knew she would be in his place. But then, she'd been raised in a crowd scene. She couldn't remember when there weren't people around. For him, life had been different.

"Nope."

"Must be nice to be so self-contained."

"It is." His tone left no room for argument.

But when she left several minutes later, Hawk found the silence disturbing.

She really was getting to him.

Chapter Nine

Claire stood behind the door, counting off the minutes. Waiting until she was sure he was gone. Then, bracing her shoulders, she opened the door again, needing to fill the small apartment with fresh air.

Needing to feel that fresh air on her skin.

Her eyes swept up and down the path that led to her garden apartment.

There was no one else around.

He'd brought the restlessness back, this man with his gray-blue eyes and his photo album. She could feel her adrenaline warming, coursing through her veins.

It made her want to cry.

She'd finally, finally reconciled with the dark hole that was at the center of her life. Finally reconciled with not ever knowing.

It was as if she'd been born fifteen years ago. Born wandering a road, her hair wet, her clothes damp and clinging to her body. Her mind had been a blank, her body filled with pain.

She'd long since given up trying to remember, other than thinking someone had to be after her. Someone who would hurt her if he ever found her.

Why else had there been so many bruises on her body? Why else had there been such a bleeding gash on her forehead?

And why else had there been such a feeling of terror inside of her, terror before her mind ever came into its hazy focus?

So she'd hidden herself. Hidden herself behind a name she'd put together from two articles in the newspaper, hidden herself inside a life she'd stitched together from the bits and pieces that came her way, never getting as close to anyone as she wanted, afraid that would be taken away from her, too.

All the while waiting for something to happen. For someone to find her.

Was this Andrew Cavanaugh the one she'd been waiting for?

She didn't know.

If he was who he said he was—her husband, the father of these children whose faces meant nothing to her—wouldn't she have remembered? Wouldn't something have been triggered inside when he looked at her?

Instead, all she felt was panic, a growing panic. And confusion.

Taking a step out to make sure he was really gone, her toe came in contact with something.

Claire looked down and saw the book the man had tried to make her take. She stared at it for a long moment, then bent down and picked it up.

She touched the pages. They were worn, as if they had been well-read. Well loved.

Flipping to the front, she saw that there was a card stuck there. And there was an inscription across the title page. *To my Rose. All my love forever, Andy.*

Andy.

She passed a hand over her forehead. The headaches were starting again. The headaches that brought with them half-formed bits of memories that refused to assume any kind of lasting shape or form.

Claire sighed, closing the book and holding it to her chest. "I wish I could remember you, Andy. I wish I could remember," she whispered to the man who wasn't there.

She took the book inside with her when she closed the door.

"Okay, Dad, what's up?" Shaw asked as he walked into the kitchen.

Behind him was Callie. He'd picked her up on his way over here. She was alone, sans her fiancé and

Brent's daughter, who had now become regulars at
the table. Their father had specifically asked that they
all come today, but without their intended mates.
From the looks of it, even their cousins seemed to be
excluded.

Everyone thought the request rather odd, especially
since Andrew liked nothing better than having the
house filled to the rafters. "The more the merrier"
applied not only to family, but to friends and even
passing acquaintances.

This was different.

This was for immediate family only.

Teri had been the first one down, followed closely
by Rayne. Clay had arrived not five minutes later.
"Looks like we're all here." Teri turned expectantly
toward her father.

Was it her imagination, or did he look paler lately?
He'd been so quiet these past two days. It wasn't like
him. Something was wrong. His behavior made her
uneasy. No matter how carefree she liked to portray
herself, she didn't like the dynamics changing within
their family. She never had.

"Yeah, what's the big mystery?" Clay pressed.
Sitting down, he helped himself to breakfast. Very
little interfered with his appetite.

On the table stood, by Andrew's standards, only a
meager offering. Pancakes and eggs with slices of
toast piled haphazardly on the side. Usually there was
at least twice as much available.

Concern entered Callie's eyes. Instead of sitting

down, she crossed to her father and placed her hand on his shoulder. "Dad, is there something wrong?"

Backing away, Andrew held his hand out, silencing his oldest daughter. He searched for words that should have been the happiest he'd ever uttered. Words that were being held prisoner because the woman he'd found, the one who he had been searching for for such a long time, didn't know him.

His eyes swept over the faces of his children, his heart growing heavier by the moment. "I found your mother."

For a second, there was nothing but silence in the normally noisy kitchen. Aching, awkward silence. They'd been here before, brought to this destination by rumors that turned out not to be true, leads that ended nowhere. It was too much to go through again.

"Dad—" Shaw began, rising from his place at the table.

Andrew waved him into silence. "No, hear me out." His voice was strained, filled with emotions he was trying to rein in.

Teri saw her brothers and sisters all exchange bewildered looks. Had it finally happened? Had looking for their mother finally taken a toll on him, pushed him over the edge? She wanted to throw her arms around him, to beg him not to do this to himself.

But even as she rose from her chair, Rayne's next question froze her in place.

"Was it that woman, Dad?" Rayne asked suddenly. "That woman at the diner?" Her eyes widened. "Did you go up to see her?"

"What woman?" Clay asked. "What diner?" He looked from one blank face to another. "Will someone please tell me what's going on?"

"Yes," Andrew replied, looking at his youngest. "I went up to see her."

"See who?" Clay demanded again.

Teri bit her lower lip. It broke her heart to see him like this. He had to give it up. "Dad, we've been through this before—"

Andrew didn't waste his time making any protests. He was a man of the law, after all, and evidence was almost always the final word. He gave it to his children now. "I matched her prints."

"What prints? Start at the beginning, please," Callie begged, giving voice to what they were all thinking.

For the past two days, he had been wrestling with this, with what he knew and what had happened when he'd gone up to see Rose, searching for a way to tell them. Wondering if he *should* tell them.

He finally came to the conclusion that they deserved to know, even if there never was a proper resolution.

"Rayne saw her first," he told them quietly, his voice throbbing with emotion. "She stopped at a diner on her way up the coast last month and was struck by this waitress working there. The woman looked just the way your mother would have if…"

His voice cracked and he cleared it, momentarily unable to continue.

Teri turned to look at her younger sister. "Why didn't you say something?" she demanded. Why had she kept this to herself? For years, all the clues, all the leads, had been made available to all of them. They'd dissected everything, always together. Why was it different now?

Rayne raised her chin defensively. "I did." She nodded toward their father. "To Dad. I thought maybe I was imagining it." She looked at him now. "But I wasn't, was I, Dad?"

"No, you weren't." Everyone started asking questions at once. He held his hand up for quiet. "I went up to see for myself and got her to leave her prints on a spoon. I took that to Claude Wilkins, had him match it against the prints on that book your mother loved so much."

"Gone with the Wind," Teri murmured almost to herself. Her pulse was racing as she listened to her father, as she hung on each unembroidered word. Unable to believe that it was true even if her heart wanted it to be. This was just another trip up the garden path, another trip that would bring them back full circle to where they'd started. Without her mother. She looked at her father, a tiny piece of information falling into place. "So that was what you were doing at the crime lab."

"Yes." He looked at each and every one of them before saying, "The prints match."

"So what are we waiting for?" Shaw was on his feet, ready to jump into his car and drive to wherever his mother was. "Why don't we go up there and get her? Why isn't she here already?"

Rayne's voice cut him off. "Because she doesn't remember us." She looked at her brothers and sisters, anguish in her eyes. "She looked right at me and didn't know who I was." Rayne's eyes shifted to her father's face. "That's it. Isn't it, Dad? She doesn't remember any of us, does she?"

"So? We'll make her remember," Clay said.

Callie shook her head, always the most practical one. "You can't force this kind of thing."

"So what?" Clay demanded. "We're just going to let her stay up there?"

"No," Andrew's voice quelled the rising tension. "We're going to give her time. I talked to her," he told his children. "Showed her photographs of all of you. Of our life."

"And?" Shaw wanted to know.

He held nothing back. "She seemed afraid. Afraid to try to remember." Each word wounded him, but he couldn't dwell on that now. He had to think positively. "I'll go back up there in a few days and try again."

Clay blew out an impatient breath. "Dad—"

"Let him handle it," Teri ordered, cutting off her twin. The words came out a little more forcefully than she'd intended, fueled by the emotions that ricocheted everywhere inside of her. "He knows what's best."

It hurt to be here, to speculate. In its own way, this was almost as bad as not knowing if her mother was alive or dead. She rose from the table. "Look, Dad, I've got to go." Feeling like someone in a trance, she crossed to her father and brushed a kiss against his cheek. "It's going to be all right," she whispered against his ear.

Andrew smiled into her eyes, knowing exactly what she was going through. Because he was going through it himself. "Funny, I was going to say the same thing to you."

She hardly remembered saying goodbye to the others before she left.

Her mother was alive.

Alive.

But if she didn't remember them, was it really her mother or just her empty shell?

What if she never remembered, never wanted to come back? What then?

Teri pressed her lips together to keep back the sob that suddenly rose in her throat. She didn't know what to do with it, what to do with what her father had just told them or with what she was feeling right now. So she just pushed it all aside until she could deal with it, clamping down a giant lid on it all.

She wasn't talking.

For once, the car wasn't filled with her endless, ebullient rhetoric. The car was silent, except for occasional static from the scanner.

Hawk frowned.

Cavanaugh had been like this since he'd first seen her this morning. Atypically quiet, withdrawn into herself the way he'd never seen her.

And it was driving him crazy.

It surprised him that he didn't find comfort in the silence. He'd always liked silence. But having it all but surrounded him except for an occasional word seemed almost unnatural. Not to mention disturbing.

They'd been on the road all day, going from one burglary victim on their list to another, asking them to try to remember their habits from five or four years back. Some had been more than a little surprised to be contacted after all this time. A few took it to mean that at least some of their things had been recovered. All had seemed irritated by what they obviously deemed irrelevant questions.

He'd left the smoothing out of ruffled feathers and sympathy up to Cavanaugh. She always handled that kind of thing well, a hell of a lot better than he could have. But as he watched her, as he listened, he had the definite impression that she was just going through the motions. That she was really somewhere else even as she mouthed the right words.

It didn't quite click into place the way it normally did.

As he began to listen more closely, Hawk thought he detected something in her voice, in her manner. It should have bothered him a great deal that he found himself so in tune to a person he was trying to keep at arm's length. But he told himself he was just being a good detective and noticing things like that was all part of the job.

If the excuse was somewhat thin, he pretended not to notice.

As the day progressed, it only got worse, not better. Cavanaugh hardly said a word over the quick sandwiches they grabbed at a take-out window. There was no annoying chatter the way there usually was, no using him as a sounding board. Nothing. She sat and ate her lunch, her eyes a million miles away.

And now, on their way back to the precinct, she made no comment that they had discovered each and every one of the victims they had visited had used a valet service to park their car within a month of the burglaries. Ordinarily, she would have been hooting over that. After all, it was her theory they'd just substantiated.

"You seem a little off today," he finally said. "Something wrong?"

She looked at him, stunned, despite her mental stupor. She didn't think there was much that Hawk could do to surprise her, but she was wrong. This definitely came under that heading. She would have bet that she could have come to work naked and as long as it didn't have any bearing on the case they were working, he wouldn't have noticed.

"No." She could feel him looking at her, as if he knew she wasn't telling him the truth. As if he expected her to own up. She wouldn't have thought that he'd cared one way or another.

"Some people are born liars." He looked back at the street. "You're not one of them."

She stared straight ahead at the darkened road. "What makes you think there's something wrong?"

He laughed at the absurdity of the question. Anyone who had ever met her would have known there was something wrong. "Well, for one thing, you're not talking a mile a minute. You're not talking at all."

More surprises. If she hadn't known better, she would have said he sounded annoyed. "I thought that was what you wanted."

He wished she'd stop blocking him like this. "Not when it means there's something wrong."

She turned to look at him, resentment coming out of nowhere and taking hold of her. "Since when do you care if there's something wrong or not?"

"Since you're my partner. As my partner, you're supposed to have my back and I have yours. That's not going to go according to plan if your head's somewhere else."

"My head's right here," she snapped at him.

If he hadn't thought something was wrong before, he would have now. "I thought you were the poster girl for sharing."

Why was he doing this to her, pretending as if he cared? "I thought you burned posters like that."

Never a patient man, he seemed to have an incredibly small supply of patience available to him at the moment. It went up in smoke. "You don't want to tell me, fine. But work out whatever's bothering you fast because right now you're deadweight."

She set her mouth hard. What else could she have expected from him? "Very compassionate of you."

That did it. Hawk pulled the car over to the side and threw it into park. He turned to face her. "I asked. You wouldn't tell. What the hell do you want from me, Cavanaugh?"

The temptation to haul off and hit him came galloping out of nowhere and it took everything she had not to act on it. What she wanted was for the world to stop tilting on its axis and straighten up again. What she wanted was to have her world back in order.

What was going on inside of her now felt just like it had when she'd heard that her mother had died. Except now the woman had been resurrected.

But not completely.

Afraid she was going to explode, Teri suddenly undid her seat belt and bolted out of the car. She went running down the block, no clue as to where she was going, only that she wanted to get away from him. From everything.

Stunned, Hawk couldn't believe what he was seeing. "What the hell are you doing? Where are you going?" he called after her.

When she didn't answer, didn't even turn around, Hawk jumped out of the car and followed her. He was concerned—more than he realized he could be. It wasn't difficult catching up to her. For one thing, his legs were a lot longer. Grabbing her by the shoulders, he spun her around to face him.

About to shout at her, he felt the words dying in his throat. There were tears shimmering in her eyes. The woman just didn't play fair.

But then, he had a feeling she wasn't playing at all. His grip on her shoulders lessened. "What's going on, Teri?" he asked in a voice that was a lot softer than what he'd just used.

She didn't want to tell him. Didn't want to tell anyone. Because this wasn't the answer to a prayer. This was an extension of a nightmare. She'd lost her mother once, and now it looked as if she was still losing her.

The words came out in a hoarse whisper. "My father found my mother."

So that was it. He felt something strange, a protectiveness uncurling inside of him. "He found her body?" he asked softly.

She shook her head. The tears she was valiantly trying to hold back spilled. "No, he found *her*. She's alive."

He didn't understand. Everyone knew about what had happened to the chief's wife. Her car had been fished out from the bottom of the river. Enough time had passed to declare her legally dead twice over. "I thought she was dead."

Teri swallowed. The ache wouldn't leave, not from her throat, not from her stomach. "I thought so, too. I didn't want to, but I finally did."

He didn't understand why she wasn't jumping up and down for joy. "Where did he find her?"

"In some diner upstate someplace. She works there, I think."

"Is he sure?"

"He's sure."

Very gently, he turned her around and started to usher her back to the car. She offered no resistance. He'd seen people suffering from shock. Now that he thought of it, she had a great many of the signs. But why? "I don't get it. If he found her, why are you like this? Why aren't you happy?"

She stopped walking just shy of the car. "She doesn't know us. Doesn't know him." There was confusion tempered with anguish in her eyes as she looked at him. "I don't know how to feel."

Now it was beginning to make sense. "Numb," he told her. He knew that would be the way he'd react if something like this had hit him.

Maybe it would be better that way, Teri thought. Better if she did just shut everything down until she could go and see her mother for herself. There was no way she was going to just leave this in abeyance, even if that was what her father wanted. It wasn't what *she* wanted.

What she wanted was to have her mother back. Whole.

He saw the look in her eyes. It was a look he'd once felt in his own soul. It'd been so long ago, it was almost hard to remember. But he did. It was a feeling of being so lost he'd felt that no one could ever find him. After a while, it had ceased to matter if someone would.

He held the car door open for her, waiting for Teri to get in. When she did, he closed the door and then got in on his side.

He paused for a moment, weighing his words before he made a decision. "Look, we're done for the day. Why don't we clock out and go somewhere for a drink?"

She shook her head. She didn't want to go to the Shannon, wasn't up to trying to pretend that everything was fine.

"Thanks, but I'll take a rain check."

That was *really* not like her, and he was starting to get worried. For all the reasons he'd cited to her and more. "Dinner, then."

She blinked, looking at him. She couldn't have heard him right. "What?"

It took effort, but he couldn't just leave her like this. "Come have dinner with me. We can talk."

The offer coaxed out the first smile he'd seen on her lips all day. "I'd like to see some ID please. My partner doesn't do dinner."

"He does when his back's on the line. Now shut up and don't argue. You're having dinner with me. And we'll talk."

"Meaning you want me to talk."

"Yeah." Out of the corner of his eyes, he saw her cock her head. "What are you doing?"

"Listening for the sounds of hell freezing over."

He figured he was on the right trail. The light had just appeared at the end of the tunnel.

Hawk smiled.

Chapter Ten

It was too early for the late crowd, too late for the early crowd. As a result, the small Mexican restaurant Hawk had brought her to was thinly populated. Only a third of their tables were in use.

She'd ordered a quesadilla. Because food was of no consequence to him one way or another, he'd ordered the same. He wasn't here to eat, but to listen.

Except that there was nothing to listen to, beyond the mild buzz of the conversation from the other tables.

Hawk gave her the first ten minutes, then said, "Okay, talk to me."

The smile that blossomed on her face stirred something within him. It was like seeing the sun come out after a long storm. She was a very pretty woman, but when she smiled, she was the closest thing to beautiful that he had ever seen. Not the kind of model-perfect beautiful that could be found on the covers of popular magazines, but a kick-in-your-gut kind of beautiful.

It took him a beat to come around. "Did I say something funny?" he asked.

"Yeah, you did." Her smile widened as she looked at him. The man was full of surprises today. "I just never thought I'd hear you say that to anyone besides a suspect—least of all me."

He shrugged, turning his attention to the cheese that oozed out from around the outer edges of the quesadilla. It was a lot safer right now than looking into her blue-gray eyes.

"Some people need to talk or they explode. You're one of them."

"Very perceptive of you." And ordinarily, he'd be right. She did feel like something was exploding inside of her, but she hadn't a clue as to how to put it into words, or even explain what she was feeling. She didn't grasp it enough to reduce it to a succinct description.

"It's called a survival mechanism." He paused, taking a bite, before continuing. "I don't want you exploding all over me."

She knew that wasn't the reason he was willing to listen to her pour out her heart now. He was doing it because beneath the gruff exterior, he was decent and kind. "Why do you act so tough?"

He raised his eyes toward her only for a moment. "Maybe because I am."

"A tough guy wouldn't have sprung for the special of the day and sat down waiting for me to spill my guts."

"You're changing the subject."

She shrugged helplessly. "Maybe because I don't know what to say."

Hawk laughed shortly. "That's a first. You'll find a way to go on talking even when they bury you."

She put down her water glass, wrinkling her nose at his comment. "There's a pleasant thought."

"I don't do pleasant thoughts, Cavanaugh. That's your department." He was almost finished eating. This was taking longer than he thought it would. And he didn't want to be at it all night. "Now you want to get this off your chest, or not?"

"Well, since you asked so nicely—"

And then she stopped, because she didn't know how to start, didn't know how to get rid of this lost feeling that had taken up residence inside of her. She felt not unlike a child who had been somehow left behind when her family moved to another city.

She switched subjects so quickly, he nearly got whiplash. "You know, in nine months, I never heard you call me Teri, except today."

That had been a slip, really. First names put them on a footing he didn't want. But she was looking at him as if she expected him to give her some kind of an answer. "Maybe because today, you looked like a Teri instead of a Cavanaugh."

Her smile deepened. So did the reaction in his gut. "And what does a 'Teri' look like?"

He said the first thing that came into his head. "Vulnerable."

"Pretty analytical for a guy who doesn't usually talk."

He moved his shoulders carelessly. "Just because I don't talk doesn't mean I'm stupid."

Had she insulted him? She didn't mean to. Teri set her glass down on the table. It was nearly empty. A waitress appeared to refill it and flash a generic smile. "How is everything?" the young woman asked as if she was preprogrammed.

"Fine," Teri assured her, then waited until the waitress retreated before looking back at Hawk. "I would have never called you stupid even if you'd never said a word."

"Then how would you know I wasn't?"

"Your eyes. You have very perceptive, probing eyes." They were also the lightest shade of ice blue she'd ever seen. And they were incredibly unsettling. Incredibly sexy. Like the man himself, something whispered inside of her. "They look as if they would see right through walls."

The image brought a half smile to his lips. "X-ray vision?"

Good, he was smiling. That meant they were out of the woods. More than half-finished with her meal, she slowed down to a crawl. She found herself not wanting the moment to end. Not wanting to leave here. Or him.

"Something like that." Tilting her head slightly, she studied him, as if she could get a better handle if she allowed her view to get off kilter. "What do you do at night, Hawk? When you walk away from the police precinct and go home for the day, what do you do?"

"This is about you, not me."

"Humor me," she urged with a smile that balanced out his frown. "It helps."

He sighed. Okay, why not? He'd opened the floor to dialogue by asking her to come here, so he had no one to blame but himself. His voice slipped into a singsong pattern "I go home. I go through the mail. I eat. I go to bed and get up the next day."

That sounded awful. "And that's it? Don't you want more?"

They were approaching the portion of the pond that was covered by thin rather than thick ice. "I have more. Between the time I come in and the time I go home, if I'm lucky, I catch bad guys." He blew out a breath, as if that signaled an end to the discussion. "Now can we get this back around to you?"

She didn't have to go into a long, linear recitation about what was bothering her to feel better. But then, he probably didn't understand that. He operated under a different set of parameters than most of the world.

"We are. Maybe you don't know this—because you think talking's a waste of time—but you don't have to talk about what's bothering you in order to feel better about it. Sometimes it just helps to kick back and be with a friend."

"Then what are you doing here?" She had friends, a whole boatload of friends. He saw the way people gravitated to her whenever they were working. She attracted people like honey brought in flies. And no doubt just as indiscriminately. But that wasn't any business of his.

"Being with a friend," she replied simply. Before he could say anything, she cut him off. "And don't deny it. If you weren't my friend, you'd be home now—" her mouth curved "—going through all that mail."

The last thing he wanted was for her to make a big deal out of this. "I already told you, as long as we're partners, I can't afford to have you mentally balancing on the hairy edge. You never know when I might actually need you."

She sighed, shaking her head. "Why is it so hard for you to accept the fact that you can be nice, that you can be normal?"

Finishing his meal, he threw his napkin onto his empty plate. "Well, my work here is done."

She didn't follow. "What?"

"You're back." He gestured toward her as if that underscored his point. "You're working at trying to pull me over to your side of the light. That means you're back on track. As annoying a pain as you ever were. Now, I've got to get home."

She made no move to rise. "Why? Junk mail calling to you?"

His cell phone rang before he could come up with an appropriate answer. For once, he was relieved to hear it ring. He heard her sigh as he flipped it open and put it to his ear. "Hawkins."

Teri tried to hear what the voice on the other end of the line was saying, but although it was loud enough for the sound to register, the words did not. She saw Hawk frown as he listened.

"Don't bother calling her. She's with me now. We'll be right there." He snapped the phone shut, terminating the call.

She couldn't read the expression on his face. "What is it?"

"That was Peter Kellerman from Homicide."

"Why's Homicide calling you?" She knew he'd transferred from Homicide, but he wasn't the type to stay in touch with anyone from his past.

Wrong. What about Jocko?

It occurred to her that there was nothing about Jack Hawkins that was a sure thing, except that he was a good cop. And a damn fine-looking man, that same annoying voice in her head whispered.

Hawk dug into his jacket pocket for his wallet and took out several bills. Looking around, he raised his hand for the waitress. "Kellerman found a couple of bodies they thought we might be interested in."

"I don't—" And then it hit her just as the waitress approached. "The two guys we caught the other day. They made bail today."

"Check, please," he said to the young woman, who nodded and retreated. He looked back at Teri. "Guess we won't have to worry about them jumping it." He gave her the particulars as Kellerman had given them to him. "They were both found knifed in an alley behind a bar on Alton Road."

It was too much of a coincidence to think it was just a random act, Teri thought. Someone was afraid that they would talk.

Any appetite she might have still had was gone.

It was a grim scene.

Both men had been eliminated by the same kind of quick slit to the throat. There was blood everywhere as it had gone shooting out. Looking at the chalk-outlined bodies, Teri stifled the shiver that threatened to shimmy up and down her spine.

"Someone *really* didn't want them to talk," she murmured to Hawk.

She moved out of the way as one of the crime scene investigators snapped photographs of the bodies. The CSI unit, comprised of three people, had arrived minutes before she and Hawk had reached the scene. They appeared to be in a world of their own, taking in every bit of evidence, no matter how minor or insignificant looking, and logging it in.

The dead men were both young. Too young to die this way. For the first time, she saw them as people rather than perpetrators or invaders. She wondered about their families and who was going to be grieving at their funerals.

Maybe the job was getting to her.

Or maybe her emotions were still too shaken up for her to make any sense out of anything that was going on.

Teri ran her hands up and down her arms. Despite her jacket, she felt cold.

"Tough break," Kellerman, a tall, easygoing gray-haired man in his late fifties, said.

"Maybe for them," Teri allowed. "But not for us." She thought of the day's work they'd just put in. Although the robbery victims used a variety of different valet services, they had all made use of that kind of service. Which meant they had a tie-in. "We've got other leads."

Kellerman looked at Hawk after giving Teri an appreciative once-over. "She always this cheerful?"

"This is when she's down." Hawk put his hand out to the other man. Kellerman shook it. "Thanks for letting us know. I want to see the M.E.'s report on them when it's done."

"Please," Teri added with a wide smile as she looked at Kellerman.

Kellerman laughed. "I'll make sure you get a copy," he promised.

Hawk walked back to his car. Teri had parked right behind him. Despite the commotion in the background coming from both the police and the handful of onlookers who had piled out of the bar to take in what was going on, he could hear her heels as they rhythmically hit the concrete.

He nodded toward the scene they'd just left. "You seem back in form."

She wouldn't exactly say she was back to normal, but she was feeling a lot better now than she had earlier. And she had him to thank for that. She stopped beside her car.

"Yeah," she agreed. "Thanks to my partner, I think I'm going to be okay now. I owe you."

He waved away the supposed debt. He didn't even want her thanks, much less have her feel as if she owed him something. "Forget it."

Rounding her trunk, she crossed to him. "No, I won't."

Hawk sighed. The line about no good deed going unpunished echoed in his head. "That's what I'm afraid of." He opened his door, ready to call it a night. "I'll see you in the morning."

He noticed that she wasn't getting into her car. That usually meant trouble.

"I'll have that drink now."

"What?"

"You asked me out for a drink earlier, remember?" she reminded him. "I took a rain check." And she wanted to collect. For some reason she wasn't about to explore, she didn't want the evening to be over. Didn't want to say good night to him.

Hawk turned his palm up toward the starless sky as if checking for drops. "I don't see any rain. Besides, you exchanged it for dinner."

"Okay—" she leaned on the edge of his car door "—then I'll buy the drink."

Hawk got in behind the steering wheel and pulled the door shut. "I'm going home."

Glancing in his rearview mirror, he saw that she

was still standing where he'd left her. Watching him.

He turned his eyes onto the road.

The edginess that had been steadily creeping over him all day continued to intensify. He'd thought that once he was away from her, it would go away.

But it didn't.

It lingered on, clinging to him like smoke. Damn it, what was going on? Why now? It didn't make any sense. The only answer he had was that her effect on him had to be cumulative.

What he needed, he thought heading to his refrigerator, was a stiff drink. Maybe two. Followed by a good night's sleep.

He doubted it would go away, but it was worth a shot.

Unbuttoning his shirt, he pulled the end out of his waistband. His service revolver and holster were on the counter by the door where he placed them every night. He paused to turn the radio on. It was set to a jazz station. A slow melody softly filled the air.

He did his best to unwind.

The knock on the door negated any progress he made. Instantly alert, he reached for his weapon before turning toward the door.

"Who is it?"

"Your partner."

What the hell was she doing here? Served him right for letting her get to him like that. He should have just ignored the anguish he'd seen on her face.

Muttering under his breath, he unlocked the door and pulled it open.

The first thing she saw was the gun. Teri raised her brows in mild surprise. "Expecting trouble?"

He put the safety back on. "It looks as if it just walked in." Placing the gun back in the holster, he turned around to look at her. "Why can't I get rid of you tonight?"

She held a brown bag up. It was tightly wrapped around a bottle. "I just came by with this to say thank you."

He took the bottle she handed him, removing the wrapper. She'd brought him Scotch.

"I heard a rumor that you liked having Scotch once in a while."

He was aware of no such rumor. Hawk placed the bottle on the counter next to his weapon. "You didn't have to do this."

He lived like a Spartan, she thought, looking around. It didn't come as a surprise. What did surprise her was that he had music on.

"And you didn't have to try to talk me down from that emotional ledge I was standing on."

"I thought you came from a family of cops, not drama queens."

In response, she merely gave him a smile. A crooked smile that went straight to his gut. This was a bad idea, he thought, letting her come in here. He should have stood his ground by the door.

Too late now.

Hands in her pockets, Teri slowly scanned the small space, all of which could have been nestled into any one of the rooms in her father's house. Except that this represented Hawk's entire apartment. A bed, a table and chair, a combination refrigerator/stove/sink, a television set sharing space with a pile of books and one love seat because there was no room for a sofa. For a big man, he didn't seem to need much space.

She turned around to face him again. "So this is where you live."

He leaned against the counter, watching her. "You already knew that or you wouldn't be here."

"From the outside," she corrected. "I knew your address, not what the place looked like." She flashed a smile at him. "So, want to give me the grand tour?"

With a resigned, less-than-patient sigh, Hawk swung his hand from one end of the room to the other. "There, you've had the grand tour."

She slid her hands into her pockets. "It's kind of small."

Hawk shrugged. He'd never needed anything fancy. And it was his, which was all that mattered. Growing up, he would have killed to have something like this. "It's got everything I need."

In this day and age of excess, it was unusual to meet someone who was satisfied with so little. The home invaders would have turned right around at the door had they targeted his place. "Don't need much, do you?"

"Nope." He pinned her with a long, penetrating look. Wanting her to leave before he made a misstep they were both going to regret. "What are you really doing here, Cavanaugh?"

So it was Cavanaugh again, not Teri, she thought. He was retreating. "Hanging out with my partner?" she offered cheerfully.

He wasn't the kind to kick back with in front of the TV with a couple of beers and they both knew it. The longer she stayed, the more dangerous the situation became. "What does it take to get rid of you?"

"I don't know." She drew closer to him. "A silver bullet?" Her eyes teased him as she lifted her chin up in an unconscious show of defiance. "What have you got?"

What he had was an overwhelming craving to kiss her. To have her.

It was all wrong and he knew it.

She was crowding him, just by standing there, by breathing. He wanted her to go before he asked her to stay. What was it that he'd once heard her say? "You're messing with the universe."

She grinned. Broadly. And he had this urge to wipe the grin from her mouth with his own. "You do listen to me when I talk," she said.

He did, a lot more than he wanted to, but he didn't want her making a big deal of it. By now, he knew her. She could make bouquets out of a single daisy. "It's like water on tile. A little of it always manages to seep through eventually no matter how good the seal is."

"Poetic and utilitarian," she observed. "There're no end to your talents, is there?"

When she breathed, he could almost feel her

breasts brushing against his rib cage. "There's an end, all right, and it should be here."

Should be, but wasn't.

She was getting to him again, getting to him with the force of a ten-ton bomb. Maybe it was the small space. She seemed to fill it just as she did the inside of the car at times. Filled it with her exuberance, with the zest that seemed to vibrate all around her.

He could feel the pull between them, drawing him in. Tempting him to cross over a line that shouldn't be crossed. He tried again. "Look, maybe you'd better go."

She made no move. "I just got here." Her voice was innocent. Tempting. "Your hosting skills need a little polishing."

"I'm not playing host." He moved a lock of her hair back, exposing her neck. Wondering what it would be like to taste the skin there. "Maybe I'm still playing your protector."

She could feel her heart hammering again, far harder than when she'd raced after the home invaders the other day. "What are you protecting me from?"

"Me."

His breath danced along her face. She felt her body tightening. Waiting. "I don't think I need any protection from you."

"Think again," he advised. He took her chin in his hand, framing her face. Desire moved in, setting up homesteading.

There was little space between them. So little space that a speck would have trouble passing through.

He knew he should step back.

One of them should hang on to good sense and it looked as if the mantle fell to him. She wasn't the kind to be warned off. But she could be frightened off.

He pulled her to him and brought his mouth down to hers—hard. For one moment, he unchained his desire. Kissed her as savagely as he could, hoping to scare her away before he wouldn't let her go.

He succeeded in scaring himself instead. Scaring himself by the way his head seemed to spin when he kissed her, by the way his blood warmed in his veins, roared in his ears.

The hunger he felt threw him. He had all the normal male urges, but this, this was different. This was something he wasn't sure if he could control.

With effort, Hawk drew his head away. She looked dazed, as if she were shell-shocked.

Run.

He didn't know if the thought applied to her, or to him.

Teri pressed her lips together, tasting him. Her heart wouldn't stop hammering.

Bewilderment filled her eyes as she looked at him. "Why did you stop?" she wanted to know. "You were just getting to the good part."

For just a moment longer, he held himself in check. "Last chance."

He was warning her. But she didn't want to be warned. Her emotions were all over the chart and she wanted to focus them. To give them a place to gather.

The tension between them felt as if it would erupt at any minute and she didn't want to wait any longer.

The sides of his shirt hung open, inviting her. She didn't turn a deaf ear. Teri spread her fingers along his chest. "I'm not going anywhere."

He laced his fingers through her hair. She felt fragile, as if he could break her into pieces if he tried. If she knew what was good for her, she'd run out of here and keep on running.

"Maybe you should."

Teri raised her chin. "You don't scare me, Jack Hawkins." Her feet were firmly planted on the floor, her body language all but daring him to make her leave. "I'm not afraid of you."

The ache inside of him was growing. "Maybe you should be."

And then he brought his mouth down on hers again.

Chapter Eleven

It was a full-scale attack.

There was no other way to regard it. Hawk was assaulting her senses, her mind, her body, just by the very act of kissing her. There was no avenue of escape.

She didn't want one.

Her body heated. It was like a fever, brought on by some small, almost undetectable source, infecting her. Spreading until it raged throughout her entire being. Raged through her until she couldn't even recognize herself.

She was like a woman possessed.

Possessed by him. Obsessed by this feeling he was creating within her.

She enjoyed life, enjoyed what it had to offer, enjoyed, when the timing was right, the intimacies that were available between a man and a woman. Those were all undertaken with an understanding. There were to be no strings. No regrets.

But there was never this storm, this passion that began almost at the very starting line, making her want to race toward the finish banner before it vanished from view. From her grasp.

Urgently, she pulled the shirt from Hawk's shoulders, bunching it down his arms as she struggled to free him from its confines. Her heart hammered harder as she felt his hands delve beneath her shirt, coming in contact with her bare skin.

Chills alternating with waves of heat shimmied up and down her spine. She felt his fingers probing, brushing against the bottom swell of her breasts.

Everything within her went on full-scale alert, even as that small shred of brain that was still clinging to logic told her to back off. To leave the liquor and take her sanity while it was still available and run. Run as fast as she could for the door and escape. Run because this time, it was different.

This time, she was in danger. In danger not just of screwing up her partnership, but her life as she knew it. As she wanted it to be.

This force had to be what her father had felt when he'd fallen for her mother. It had driven him all those years he tried to find her, even as everyone else told him to give it up. Love made him continue.

Love, she'd felt, that had almost destroyed him.

And yet, her father had found her mother. Love had given him the will, the stamina, the courage to keep on against all odds. Love had been his beacon.

What was she thinking? Love? What love? What was happening here wasn't love, it was sex, attraction to the nth degree, desire run amok, nothing else, nothing more.

It was enough. *For now.*

She wanted Hawk with a craving she hadn't thought possible. Each touch, each kiss drew her in, blotting out all reason. She wanted him.

"You won't be needing this," Hawk murmured against her mouth.

Needing what? My mind? Too late. It's already gone.

The next moment, Hawk was backing away from her, unbuckling her holster. For the first time in her life, she saw his hands look unsteady. Or was that just her trembling? No, it couldn't be that, she didn't tremble. She wasn't afraid.

And yet…

She was more afraid than she'd ever been in her whole life.

His arm brushed against her breasts as he finished removing her weapon and holster. Everything tightened inside of her, like a string across a violin bow, drawn so tightly she thought she was going to snap in half.

Anticipation hummed so loudly in her ears, she was afraid he would hear it.

Teri watched him set the weapon aside on the counter, beside his.

Just like at home.

The thought came out of nowhere, blossoming. Making her warm.

And then there was no more time to revel in tenderness.

Hawk dragged her shirt from her body, wasting little time on her bra. The hook opened, the material slid and he drew her to him in a hot embrace. Skin against naked, heated skin.

Demands slammed into each other, the rest of their clothing disappeared in a tangled puff of smoke generated by desire, by passion, by the sheer force of wills coming together.

And then he surprised her again.

He slowed down. To explore, to caress, to anoint. Hawk held her hands above her head as he made himself achingly familiar with every part of her, taking her prisoner even as he himself was imprisoned.

She twisted and turned beneath the warmth of his mouth, the heat of his gaze. With each pass of his tongue, his hot breath, she felt she died a little by inches, ready to endure death by exquisite torture.

And then her will rose to the surface. It wasn't in her nature to merely be a recipient, to take without giving. Her independence took over.

Breaking free, Teri pushed the man who had

shaken the very foundations of her existence back on the bed. Straddling him, she leaned over Hawk until her breasts just barely brushed against his chest, her hair tickling his skin, her breath destroying his resolve.

With slow, deliberate motions, she took the time to feast on his neck, savoring the dark tastes she discovered. Everything was a revelation, an adventure of the highest degree. She heard his breath shortening, becoming labored as she pressed her lips to his flesh. This reaction empowered her even as it chained her to him.

She began her own road to exploration, her fingers seeking out every part of him, her lips following the trail that had been forged. Exciting herself even as she strove to excite him.

She was driving him out of his mind.

This wasn't a planned seduction, or even an unplanned one. But since it was happening, Hawk was accustomed to having the upper hand. That he didn't here, that this slip of a woman held him in the palm of her hand from the moment she'd turned her mouth up to his, scared the hell out of him.

But he couldn't seem to pull back, couldn't force himself to break free no matter how much he counseled himself to do it. And that scared him even more. Scared him because it gave Teri Cavanaugh power over him. And if she had power, she could abuse it. Could render him helpless.

He couldn't allow that.

He couldn't stop it.

At least, not yet. Later, he'd get up and pick up all the pieces, reconstructing himself, making himself into what he'd been less than half a hour ago. For now, he wanted to enjoy her, to enjoy this sensation Teri created inside of him, this excitement that seemed to be heightening with each and every second that passed.

He'd reined himself in to prove to himself that this had no real power over him. That he was in control, could change the tempo whenever he wanted. Could even walk away if he so chose.

But all he'd managed to do was get himself more tightly trapped—like someone fighting against quicksand. The more he struggled, the deeper he sank.

He didn't care.

Not now.

Later, he'd care. Later there would be damage control and fences to urgently mend. Right now, there was only her, only this wild magical flame that burned far brighter than anything he'd ever experienced before.

Watching Teri out of the corner of his eye, he brought her up to a climax, not once, but several times, as if to prove to himself that he could. But this made him want her more.

Like the drugs he'd sworn he'd never touch, the drugs that destroyed his parents long before their deaths, one taste only made him want more. Need more. Crave more.

Controls disintegrated.

He could hear her breathing hard, trying to catch her breath.

Or was that him?

The sounds mingled, becoming one. He wanted to do the same. He couldn't hold himself back any longer. It was time.

Hawk pulled himself up over her body, brushing along the length of her, his eyes fastened to hers. With his knee, he moved her legs apart.

His pulse went erratic as he felt her legs encircle his.

With a guttural cry escaping his lips, he drove himself into her, hard, fast. Teri tightened her arms around him, welcoming him. Making him want her even more and not knowing how the hell that could be humanly possible.

The dance began. The wild, torrid dance destined to reach the stars that revolved in her head. She clung to him, to the ever-increasing tempo, to the ever-growing yearning for the final explosion.

And then it came.

The surprise, the wonder of the intensity made her cry out—she had no idea what. The euphoria came, wrapped up in exhaustion. Her heart felt as if it were going to burst through her chest.

She felt his weight slacken and then felt him slide from her body. She wanted to curl up against him. Was that weakness? She didn't know, didn't care.

MARIE FERRARELLA 177

Rather than analyze, than worry, she curled her body against his.

He hesitated for a moment, reason returning in slow dribbles and drabs. The first thought that echoed through his brain was This is wrong.

But even this thought was singed in the fire that still moved through his body, still smoldered, unwilling to be completely extinguished.

What the hell had just happened here? He'd been all but castrated and he was grinning to himself. At least inwardly. The energy required to smile outwardly eluded him at the moment.

He couldn't resist the way she curled into him. He knew he should, for his own self-preservation, but he couldn't. He wasn't strong enough yet. So he slipped his arm around her and held her to him.

Teri rested her head against his chest. He could feel each breath she exhaled as it moved along his skin, a silent, unwitting invitation.

He could feel the remnants of desire glowing in the ashes that had once been his resolve.

Damn, he wanted her again. Barely recovered and he wanted her again.

He had to be losing his mind.

"Well, this is a first," he murmured.

She raised her head to look at him just then, amusement playing along her lips. He had an urge to wipe the smile off her face with the only resource he had available. His own mouth.

"Don't tell me you're a virgin," she teased. "Because if you are, that's the best display of raw talent the world has ever encountered."

Had she just told him that he'd rocked her world the way she had his? Or was she putting him on? He never knew how to read her.

Mischief danced in her eyes. Why hadn't he noticed how bright they were, how they could delve into him?

"No." He shifted a strand of her hair through his fingers. "But I've never slept with my partner before."

"You still haven't." She saw him look at her quizzically. "As I recall, absolutely no sleeping took place."

He laughed softly. No, no sleeping took place. "You know what I mean."

"No," she said quite honestly. "I don't know what anything means right now." She sighed as if all the air was being drained out of her. "Because up is down and black is white and the whole damn world has just turned sideways on its axis." She punctuated her statement by pressing a kiss to his chest.

She saw what looked like desire taking root in his eyes.

Hawk dove his fingers through her hair, cupping her head back just a fraction. His voice was low. "It was pretty much that way for me, too."

Something stirred within her she was really afraid to put a name to, negating all her silence assurances to herself about what she was feeling. "Oh, damn,

Hawk. Just when I think I've got you all figured out, you throw me a curve like this one.''

He smiled into her eyes, his hand trailing along the swell and dip of her body. Feeling stirred in his own. Desire galvanized him. "How do you feel about catching another one?"

He saw the laughter in her eyes, coupled with surprise. Felt desire springing up in his loins. "You ready to throw another one so soon?"

He pulled her closer to him still. "Try me."

His body was hard from wanting. Her own moistened in preparation. The real world with its regrets, with its consequences, was left behind. She didn't want to think now any more than she had before. She just wanted to feel as if she were on fire again.

"I have tried you."

"And?"

Her eyes smiled into his. "Please, sir, I want some more.''

He vaguely recognized it as a quote from *Oliver Twist.* It was the last thought to pass through his mind for quite some time.

More exhausted than she thought was humanly possible, Teri finally made the effort to move out of the circle of his arms.

It was time for her to go home.

She looked around. The good thing about his having a studio was that her clothes weren't difficult to locate. The sooner she got them on, the more prepared she would be for when the awkwardness descended over her.

The awkwardness she was certain was going to follow.

So far, he hadn't said a word. Had let her get up out of the bed. Had watched her gather her clothes up and begin to get dressed.

Teri started to feel as if he wasn't going to say a word until after she left, if then.

"So where does this put us?"

So much for predictions. She turned around from the edge of the bed and looked at him. She tried to read his expression. Tried to read her own feelings, as well. Nothing straightforward arose. She felt as if she'd fallen headlong into a whirlpool and couldn't make sense of anything.

"Working on the home invasion case," she replied glibly as she continued putting on her clothes. It seemed like the safest answer at the moment.

He sat up, the sheet pooling below his navel. He didn't seem to notice. His attention was focused on the blonde tornado who had just upended life as he knew it. "That's not what I meant."

"I know what you meant." She pulled on her skirt, rising to fasten it at her waist. She addressed a spot on the opposite wall rather than look at him. "Don't worry, Hawkins, I'm not one of those women who demands a commitment when a guy brings her a flower."

She heard him laugh shortly. "That was a hell of a lot more than a flower."

She turned to look at him then, a grin playing on her lips even though she'd promised herself to keep this retreat short and sweet.

"Okay, a bouquet. A very large bouquet," she amended after a beat. She tried very hard to keep this on a footing she thought he'd appreciate. A footing she usually wanted herself.

But not this time.

"We're adults." She shrugged before buttoning up her blouse. "Things happen. End of story." She tried to get a handle on what he was thinking. What most men in his position probably thought. "Don't look so worried, I'm not about to drag out a wedding dress or a palimony contract for you to sign. We were partners before I came here and we'll be partners when I leave." Damn, but he was impossible to read. He should have looked relieved right now, but he didn't. "Why? Do you want more?"

Not with a woman as glib as her. Not with anyone, he reminded himself. "No." The word tasted harsh, unpalatable. Lies always did.

"Good, because neither do I." Even as she said it, she could feel the words hurting her.

That's because they were a lie. Weren't they? Confusion took up residence in her brain. She'd known what she was getting into even as she stood on his doorstep, waiting for him to open the door. Knew in her heart this was what she wanted. One night with him, just one night. To satisfy her curiosity. She'd hoped that one red-hot, sizzling go-round with Hawk would answer all the questions she had, would get him out of her system.

All it managed to do was get him more entrenched into it.

The old saying about best-laid plans of mice and men, she thought disparagingly, obviously also applied to women. Dressed, she looked around to see if she'd forgotten anything.

Yes, you forgot to stay out.

She took a deep breath and went to the door. "So I'll see you tomorrow?"

Hawk rose, completely unmindful of the fact that he was magnificently naked. He crossed the small room and walked over to her.

"Today," he corrected. "You'll see me today."

She could feel herself reacting again, could feel the tips of her fingers itching to touch him. To begin the process all over again. What was going on here?

Struggling to be as disinterested, as detached as he seemed, she glanced at her wristwatch.

"That's right, it's today, isn't it?" Her throat felt raspy, dry. She warned herself not to swallow like some shaky teenager. She'd seen male bodies before, seen his just moments earlier. So why was she feeling so weak-kneed again? "I didn't realize it was so late."

It was late, all right. Later than he thought. He

should have stopped what was happening before it had gotten out of hand.

He had to stop it now, before it took him over. "Give me a minute to get dressed and I'll walk you to your car."

"You don't have to." She raised her chin. "Just because we made love doesn't mean I've suddenly turned helpless."

It wasn't up for debate. And he didn't want her winning every encounter they had, even one as small as this one.

"I said I'll walk you to your car." He fairly growled out the words.

She felt her temper slipping. Maybe it was because she needed to exercise some kind of control, even over something as tiny as this. She felt as if he'd completely overwhelmed her, body and soul. "You always this cheerful after you make love?"

His eyes slitted. "We didn't make love, Cavanaugh. We had sex."

He was right and she should have gone with it, should have agreed, but her stubborn nature came to the fore, fueled by something akin to hurt. Even if she referred to it as that herself, she didn't want him denigrating what just happened.

"You had what you had and I had what I had," she told him coldly. "I'm not asking for a commitment, Hawk, but I am asking you to be civil."

"I *am* being civil."

She went toe-to-toe with him, desperately trying to

ignore the fact that he wasn't wearing anything and that it was really taking its toll on her. "Then why are you shouting at me?"

"Because I don't want you to leave," he shouted even more loudly.

That completely threw her. She scrambled to recover. "And shouting at me is going to make me stay?"

"No," he snapped. "It'll make you leave before I can make you stay."

She tried not to think about what that meant, only that she needed him to understand something. Everything else hung on this one truth.

"Let's get something straight, partner. You can't 'make' me do anything. What happens here, what happens anywhere, is my doing, as well. Hence the word *partner* instead of *flunky* or *slave*. Got that?"

He said nothing, only took hold of her shoulders, bringing her closer to him. She could feel her heart starting up all over again, could feel her body priming. "I guess I should have let you walk me to the car when I had a chance."

His eyes were fierce as Hawk felt the trap snapping shut around him again. "What makes you think you had a chance?"

She knew she was supposed to argue against his assumption, but she didn't want to. What she wanted was what he had to offer.

Her purse slipped from her fingers as she stood up

on her toes and wrapped her arms around his neck. "No fair. You're already dressed for the occasion."

He smoothed her hair away from her face, wanting just to look at her. "That can be remedied."

And it was. Quickly.

Chapter Twelve

Taking a break, Teri looked at Hawk over the rim of her coffee mug. For most of the morning, she and he had been cross-referencing information, searching for a connection, a name, something to hang their newest theory on.

A headache formed over the bridge of her nose and she paused to massage it, her eyes never leaving the top of Hawk's head. He was busy poring over something. Intent. Focused.

Unlike her. Her mind bounced back and forth like a ball at zero gravity, going from their case to the night they'd spent together.

She didn't want to feel this way, this happy-glad-Fourth-of-July-sparkler sort of way every time she thought of him. What she wanted, or felt she wanted, didn't seem to enter into it.

The sparkler continued to burn.

For the first time in her life, she had feelings, potentially deep feelings for someone—if she allowed herself to admit it—and it worried her. More than that, it frightened her. She'd seen what really loving someone could do. She only had to look to her father if the memory began to fade a little. She'd watched what he endured when he'd lost her mother. Her disappearance created a hole in his life, a hole that nothing could really fill. Despite all the love that abounded in their house, in their family, at bottom Andrew Cavanaugh was still lonely for his wife.

She didn't want that happening to her, didn't want to love someone so much that it hurt to breathe, that it cast a shadow on everything else.

And yet she knew she was on that kind of a path if she didn't somehow manage to stop herself. For all her optimism, she knew that Jack Hawkins wasn't the kind of man who allowed himself to be tied down. Home and hearth were not his kind of thing.

If she fell in love with him, she was only setting herself up for her father's kind of heartache.

It wasn't going to happen, she promised herself. It wasn't.

With effort, Teri forced herself to get back to the stack of files on her desk. She wasn't getting paid to pine, she was getting paid to solve a crime.

It felt different.

The air, the day, the office, his skin—they all felt different this morning. As if he'd just turned onto a new page, a new chapter. A new book.

Shuffling through files he wasn't completely focused on, Hawk frowned to himself.

What the hell was going on? He wasn't the type to think this way, to feel this way. To feel at all. Feelings were for people who had a prayer of leading regular lives. From the first moment he'd opened his eyes, a heroin-addicted baby born to two people who had no business procreating, his life had been anything but regular. There'd been times, when he was very young, when he'd dreamed of that life. Of actually being normal with normal parents.

But that dream had faded a very long time ago. There was no reason for it to be raising its head now, peering into his existence and whispering ever so seductively in his ear.

He didn't believe in things like that. In feelings. In people like Teri Cavanaugh who seemed to have no hidden agendas. It made him almost angry to be placed in this kind of a position, to be sitting here and wrestling with emotions he was uncomfortable with—not to mention totally unfamiliar with.

She'd opened a door inside of him, a door to a place he hadn't even suspected existed. It hadn't happened just with the sex, because it hadn't been just about sex, no matter how much each one of them denied this. It had been more.

He didn't have an explanation. He only knew that

he didn't feel like himself. Shades of gray seeped into his black-and-white world. Not just gray, but a soft sheen of colors, as well. Colors that came along with waves of confusion that washed over him. Most confusing was that she asked nothing of him, wanted nothing.

It made him want to give her everything.

Except that he knew he had nothing to give. His parents had seen to that.

He was a walking, breathing empty shell, masquerading as a person.

It had been two days since they'd been together in his apartment. Two days, two nights and a great deal of endless time in between. Time that had been filled with work, with following up leads and with trying to find the name of someone who had at one time or other worked in all or most of the valet services that seemed to be implicated. Time in which his mind was only half on the job.

And half on her.

He scrubbed his hands over his face, wishing he'd never left Homicide. Edmunds had never lingered on his mind this way.

The hairs on the back of his neck stood up. Hawk raised his eyes. She was watching him. He had the feeling she'd been doing it for quite a while now. Was she feeling restless, too? He couldn't tell.

"You're awfully quiet—for you," Hawk tacked on. "What's up?"

"This is a first, isn't it? You wanting to know if something was bothering me."

Belatedly, she'd remembered that it wasn't, that he'd tried to get at the root of what was bothering her the day they'd wound up making love. Her brain was so addled, she'd forgotten. She had to get a grip before she fell completely apart.

"It's been a week for firsts," he commented. Then, thinking that he might have given too much away, redirected her thoughts to the case. "You don't normally chew on things and keep them to yourself." He nodded toward her desk. "Find anything?"

"A hell of a lot more than I bargained for," she muttered under her breath. By the look on his face, Teri realized that the comment had slipped out when she'd meant it to be internalized. Damn, she was going to have to watch that.

"Would you like to share that with the class?"

The question came from behind her. Teri swung her chair around to find herself looking up at a worn-down-at-the-heels-looking Mulrooney. Even the doughnut in his hand looked droopy. The dead ends in the case were taking their toll.

Glancing to her left, Teri's eyes met Hawk's. Her mind scrambled for something plausible to say. "Just that beyond the common thread of all the victims having used valet services sometime before the burglaries or home invasions occurred, there doesn't seem to be anything that links up." She looked at the list of valet services, some of which had gone out of business.

"The services aren't owned by a single parent company and there hasn't been anyone who's worked at most, much less all of them."

"Maybe there doesn't have to be," Hawk ventured. Getting up, he came around to her desk. Teri suddenly felt hemmed in. "Maybe it's a group effort. Four or five friends all coordinating from their various valet services."

Teri thought of the two dead bodies in the alley. "Some friends."

"Oh, great," Mulrooney groaned, polishing off his snack. He crumpled the napkin and tossed it into her trash basket. "So what, we stake out—" he paused to count the names on Teri's list "—twelve different services?" He offered them a beefy frown. "The chief's never going to give us the manpower to do that."

"No," Hawk agreed, his mind racing ahead. "But we can get a court order to let us get access to the forms all the employees filled out when they were applying for the job. Maybe there's a common name given as a reference. He might be our key player." Mulrooney groaned again, louder this time. Hawk shot him a dark look. "It's worth a shot. We've got nothing else."

Teri raised her eyes innocently to his face. "Do we really want to wait for a court order?"

Hawk ignored the strange feeling stirring in his gut when she looked up at him like that. "You got a better idea?"

Teri glanced toward the captain's glass office. It was at the end of the squad room. Right now, the captain looked busy with his work, but she was taking no chances. "I do if you watch my back."

Mulrooney caught on and grinned widely at Hawk. "She's going to do her thing again, isn't she? She's going to hack into their systems."

The former chief's daughter or not, hacking wasn't something that was smiled upon. Hawk looked at the other man sharply. "Why don't you try standing on the roof and making that announcement?"

Mulrooney was slow to anger, but there was definite simmering going on. "Hey, what crawled up your butt and died?"

Looking to avert any escalation, Teri came to his rescue. "He's just edgy because we haven't solved it yet. Right, Hawk?"

"Yeah, right," he bit off.

"Hey, we all want this thing wrapped up," Mulrooney said good-naturedly. He glanced down at Teri. "Need me to do anything?"

"Your desk is closer to the captain's office than Hawk's is. Find a way to give me a warning if you see him coming my way." Pausing for a moment, she glanced over her shoulder at the big man. "This is going to take some time."

"Gotcha." With a smart salute, Mulrooney went back to his desk.

For a second, nothing was heard in the immediate area except for the sound of keys being tapped. Hawk glanced around. Most of the squad room was empty. The teams were all working on other cases. But there was still the network system that could easily be accessed to see what every computer in the precinct was doing. She was doing something risky and, depending on who caught her, it could carry stiff penalties and consequences.

"You know," Hawk observed, trying to sound disinterested, "for someone whose whole family is in law enforcement, you don't exactly tread the straight and narrow path."

She didn't answer him right away. Instead, afraid she might lose the thread, she waited until she completed typing in a sequence. And then she murmured, "Patience isn't."

"Patience isn't what?"

Teri looked up and smiled at him. "My cousin Patience," she clarified. "She isn't in law enforcement. She's a vet."

Damn it. The woman's smile was going straight to his gut. That wasn't normal and he didn't like it. "I'll try to remember that the next time I need a rabies shot," he grumbled. And then he replayed her comment to him. It didn't make sense. "Why do you feel you had to share that with me?"

Mentally she counted off another sequence before typing it in. "So you'll know when you come over for breakfast tomorrow."

"Come over for breakfast tomorrow?" It made no more sense to him when he said it that when she did.

"What are you talking about? I didn't agree to anything. I haven't lost that bet yet," he reminded her.

Teri didn't even look up. Her fingers continued to fly across the keyboard. He was surprised that she could even think of anything else beyond the codes she typed. The woman gave new meaning to *multitasking*. "No, but you will. There's a connection here between all the robberies and we both know it. Besides, it's time you met the rest of my family."

His eyebrows drew together. He didn't like the sound of that. Hawk bent over so that he was close to her ear. He didn't want to take a chance of anyone else overhearing. "Hey, we only slept together once. That doesn't mean I'm about to meet with your father and exchange a dozen war ponies for your hand."

God, he was jumpy, wasn't he? And because he was, she felt an inner calm rising up out of nowhere. "No ponies, no hand, Hawk, just a lot of food and conversation. You're my partner," she pointed out. "Partners get brought to breakfast, or lunch, or dinner if you prefer, although breakfast is the most common time. It also has a built-in time limit you might like because we all have to dash off to work. Well, all except Dad, of course, but then—"

He had to stop her before she got a second wind. There was no way he was going to go and meet her family under any pretext. "I don't do breakfast."

Stopping in midword, she looked up and pinned him with a look that would have made a lesser man squirm. "You do coffee. You can sit and sip."

He snorted at the idea. "Why would I want to do that?"

"Because you do." She couldn't begin to explain it any better than that. It was the way things were done, had always been done. Anyone who figured prominently into any of their lives was brought around for viewing. Time changed nothing. Her father still wanted to know the people in her life, in all his children's lives. Hawk, she could see, still waited for more. She added only two words. "Trust me."

He trusted her to watch his back, but there was no way he was going to allow her access to any other part of him. That night in his apartment had already created havoc inside of him.

If he were honest with himself, the groundwork for that havoc went back further than two nights ago. Still, the word *no* didn't come when called. Instead, he heard himself muttering, "We'll see."

Teri grinned at him. "Don't forget. I know where you live."

"So you'll come and get me?"

She still looked at him even though her fingers flew along the keyboard. "Either that, or bring everyone to you."

Hawk laughed shortly, shaking his head. "They wouldn't fit."

"My family is surprisingly resourceful. Seven-thirty would be good," she told him, lowering her eyes to the screen again.

She heard Hawk sigh and smiled to herself.

* * *

He wasn't going to show. There was no earthly reason for him to turn up at her house, he thought. He'd go into the precinct the way he'd done every other morning.

Except that he knew in his gut that if he didn't show up for breakfast, Cavanaugh wouldn't give him any peace, and if there was one thing that woman knew how to do, it was to mercilessly nudge at a man until he literally and figuratively screamed "uncle."

Like a tropical storm pounding a beach, the woman was relentless. He'd seen her in action. It would be easier just to show up.

Resigned, Hawk drove to the Cavanaugh house. With myriad cars parked in front of it and around it, the house was hard to miss. It looked more like the scene of a party than breakfast.

He fought the temptation to turn around and driving out of the development. Finally, he parked down the block and walked up to the front door.

She answered on his first ring. He wasn't even sure if he made complete contact with the doorbell before the door swung open.

"You came."

The house gave off an aura of warmth. Somewhere inside of him, where a tiny part of the small boy he'd once been still lived, came the thought that he would have liked growing up here. He envied her. And then he buried the thought.

MARIE FERRARELLA   197

"I figured I'd save myself a lot of grief." He
looked down at her. "But just this once."

"Just this once," she agreed cheerfully. "They all
have good memories," she assured him, referring to
her family. "Once is all they'll need." Urging him
on, she walked into the busy, noisy kitchen a step
ahead of him. Teri raised her voice in order to be
heard. "Everyone, this is my partner, Jack Hawkins."

Sixteen sets of eyes turned and looked in his direction. Most of the women, he noticed, were blond
like Teri. The men were all dark-haired and except
for two, looked incredibly similar. It was easy to see
that most of them were related.

For someone who'd been alone for as long as he
had, the scene was a little overwhelming. He'd never
seen a table that big before outside of a banquet hall
or a conference room. And every place, save three,
was filled. The head of the table and two chairs to the
right of that.

"Here, take a seat," Teri urged, gesturing to one
of the two chairs that were side by side.

Feeling awkward and out of place, Hawk chose the
one that was to the right of the head of the table. A
tall, distinguished-looking man in a white chef's
apron crossed to him. The man paused to wipe his
hands on the apron before extending his hand.

"Andrew Cavanaugh. Nice to finally meet you."

The handshake was firm, powerful, accepting. "I
know who you are, Chief."

"It's 'chef' now." Andrew grinned, gesturing toward the professional stove against the back wall. His children had all chipped in and bought it for him for his last birthday. "I've dropped the *i*."

"The hell he has." To his right, Hawk saw a younger version of the chief rising from his seat to take his hand. Shaw, wasn't it?

"Nice to see you again." Shaw nodded at him. Amusement played on his rugged face. "So, you're ready to meet the others?"

"Here, let me do this," Teri said, cutting in. "It'll be faster."

Clay laughed. "That's only because you have the fastest mouth."

Teri gestured toward him. "You've just heard from Clay, my little brother—"

"By five minutes," Clay pointed out. The protest was automatic. Ever since they'd been little, Teri had taken great glee in calling herself the older one.

"I was referring to maturity," Teri clarified. She went around the table. "Next to Clay is Ilene, his fiancée, poor lady, and their son, Alex." She glanced at Hawk, but there was no curiosity there. No need to know details. He was a rare man, she thought. "You've already met my older sister, Callie. Beside her is Judge Brenton Montgomery and his daughter, Rachel." She purposely left their relationship unstated, although they were slated to get married soon. Again, there was no sign that Hawk was even mildly curious as to the nature of their relationship. The man wasn't human, she decided. "My baby sister,

Rayne—'' Rayne rolled her eyes at the description ''—and Cole Garrison, who for some reason wants to marry her.''

She gestured toward the other side of the table. ''And these are my cousins, Patrick and Patience— their dad was my uncle Mike Cavanaugh.''

The reason she was afraid of hospitals, Hawk thought, nodding his head at the duo.

''And next to them,'' she was saying, ''are Dax, Troy, Jarrod and Janelle, Uncle Brian's kids. Uncle Brian couldn't make it this morning.''

At this point, Hawk found himself fervently wishing that he hadn't been able to, either. He looked at her as he took his place at the table. ''Neither could the partners, I take it.''

Teri ignored the curious look Shaw gave her. ''We ran out of room,'' she explained glibly. ''Temporarily.''

''Is that how she got you to come?'' Shaw asked. ''By telling you that our partners would be here?''

''Actually, they are, you know,'' Clay put in, looking at Ilene. ''Life partners.'' He looked back at Hawk. ''Different emphasis.''

Andrew decided it was time to get his daughter off the hook she was wiggling on. Placing a hand on Hawk's shoulder, he put down a plate of Belgian waffles in front of him. He noted that the younger man's shoulder was military rigid. Andrew began to draw his own conclusions. ''She really brought you here because I was curious about her partner. I got to meet her first partner the second day on the job.''

''Was he filing a complaint?'' Hawk asked dryly.

Andrew returned to the stove. The eggs needed to be turned. ''Matter of fact, he was asking for ear plugs, as I recall.''

She hadn't asked Hawk to come here just to hear her being teased. ''No, he wasn't.''

''Well, he would have except that he was too polite. I thought the least I could do was feed the poor guy, seeing as how he was stuck in a squad car with Teri for eight hours a day.'' Andrew looked over his shoulder toward Hawk. ''How about you—you want earplugs?''

Someone pressed a container of maple syrup into his hands. Taking it, Hawk covered the waffles sparingly. ''I've learned how to tune her out for the most part.''

''Hey, do you give lessons?'' Clay asked, his eyes gleaming. ''Because the rest of us have never managed to be able to do that.''

''You just watch her lips move and think of something else.'' The way he'd been struggling to do for the last two days. To think of anything else except the way her lips had felt against his. The way she had felt against him. So far, he was only succeeding marginally.

He didn't notice that his remark was met with a smattering of laughter.

"Thanks, I think I'll try that," one of her cousins said.

"I think I like this guy," Clay told Teri with an approving nod in Hawk's direction.

Andrew noticed that rather than making a flippant retort in response to her twin's jibe, his middle daughter was strangely quiet. Becoming mildly pensive, he took a longer, harder look at the man she'd brought to his table. There were friends to call and questions to ask.

Even though, for the most part, he trusted his children's judgment, it never hurt to examine the facts from all sides. Never hurt to be sure. Being a father rather than being a policeman had taught him that.

Chapter Thirteen

"I got it!" Excitement quickly obliterated the drowsy state that had begun to descend over her. Teri looked up from the screen where her eyes had been glued for the better part of the morning. She searched for someone to tell about the elusive connection she'd found. "I got it!" she cried again.

Deeply entrenched in thoughts that he couldn't seem to easily shake off no matter how hard he tried, Hawk raised his head and looked in her direction. She'd been rattling around in his head and there appeared to be no signs of stopping.

"Anything I can catch?"

Not even his sarcastic question could shake the high she was feeling. She'd found the damn thread. "No, but maybe Danny Tierney is."

The name hit him with the force of a bullet fired at close range. "Tierney," he repeated slowly. "Danny Tierney?"

A small fraction of her excitement abated, giving way to something more personal. To a stirring of concern. There was an odd look on Hawk's face she couldn't begin to read. "Yeah. You said the name as if you know him. Do you?"

Hawk hardened his jaw. He'd known Tierney. Once. They'd shared a small portion of his life that he was far from proud of. "I thought he went straight."

He hadn't answered her directly, but what did she expect? "Then you do know him."

"Knew him," Hawk corrected tersely. "A long time ago."

She studied his face. "About the same time you knew Jocko?"

"No, later." He was already saying too much, opening up too much. And it was all her fault. "What are you, writing a biography for me?"

Teri raised her hands innocently, as if to show him that she had nothing up her sleeves. "Just trying to piece things together about my partner—nothing else." She got back to the case and the best lead they'd come up with so far. "Would you know where we could find him?"

There were contacts he could touch, places he could look. But the Danny Tierney he'd known had been a happy-go-lucky character who would have never blown away two people to cover his own trail.

Getting up, he rounded his desk and came around to hers. Maybe, in the end, this would wind up being just another dead end.

"Not anymore," Hawk replied briskly. "How'd his name come up?"

He stood right behind her, looking at the screen. Teri moved to the right to give him a better view. She'd taken the information she'd hacked into yesterday, downloaded all the files and placed them into an empty folder, then spent the morning reading through the vast number of job applications from the combined valet services. The turnover at these places was overwhelming, but finally, a single name had cropped up, cited under the section marked "references" on various applicants' employment forms.

She pointed to it on the current application she was reading. "He keeps coming up as a reference. So far, I've seen his name twelve times."

"How many applications—a hundred?"

His voice was solemn, dead. She couldn't get a reading on his feelings.

"Try three hundred. The only thing that seems to have a faster turnaround than working at a valet service are the kids behind the counter at fast-food places and my local video store." She paused to highlight a line on the screen. "There's a phone number here. We can get an address from the reverse phone book."

Hawk nodded grimly. If confronting people from

his past gave him a problem, he shouldn't have become a cop, he told himself. He always knew there would be a crossover margin, with shadows of his past life casting themselves over to his present one.

"What are we waiting for?" he said.

Swinging her chair around, Teri griped the armrests as she rose to her feet. His expression was still the same. Still troubled. Mentally, he was chewing on something. "Is there anything you want to share with me?"

She was the last person he wanted to talk to about anything. "No."

"Okay—" she nodded gamely "—let me rephrase that. Is there anything you don't want to share with me, but should?"

Maybe this was another Danny Tierney. It wasn't as if it was the most unique name in the world. "Don't let's get ahead of ourselves."

"Ahead? I'm just trying to stay even, that's all." She tried to make him understand where she was coming from. The man clearly needed a road map. "I want to know if you and this Danny character have a history that's going to bother you."

He resented the implication. His temper flared a little too quickly. "It's not going to get in the way of doing my job," he snapped.

"That's not what I said. I specifically used the word *bother*."

He was in no mood for this, for her probing, well-intentioned or not. He didn't want her burrowing into his life, making herself comfortable, making herself at home. If he couldn't have her out of his life—his professional life—he at least wanted her out of his head.

"You know what bothers me?" he demanded, then lowered his voice to keep from attracting the attention of the other detectives in the room. "Partners who don't know when to stop talking—that's what bothers me."

She'd hit some kind of a nerve. "Old news."

"Apparently not the kind you reread."

She sighed, finding that she had to struggle to hang on to her own temper. She needed a little space herself. "I'll see about getting the address," she told him, heading for the door.

"Cavanaugh?" Teri debated just continuing out, but then she turned around. Waiting. He squeezed the word out after a beat. "Sorry."

She made no comment, merely nodded, pretending the incident was already forgotten.

But it wasn't. Hawk had been acting like a cat on a hot tin roof even before she'd had him come to breakfast. Ever since they'd made love, she realized. And at this point, his gruffness had all but gone through the roof. She'd hoped that once he'd met her family, he would mellow out just a little. Her family had that kind of effect on people, pulling them into a group situation, making them feel as if they weren't alone.

Maybe Hawk liked being alone.

No, that was wrong, she silently insisted. Nobody really liked being alone. She just had to be patient, that was all. Miracles took time, she reminded herself as she turned down the hall. And this man definitely needed one.

In the end, after months of following scraps of information that led nowhere, the investigation went down simply enough. They tracked down the former and present employees who had used Danny Tierney as their reference on the job application forms and questioned them one by one.

The fourth one, a skinny, nervous kid just fresh out of college, named Phil Sherman, broke relatively quickly. The threat of jail time had him singing loud and clear, citing names, implicating Tierney in exchange for the promise of a lenient sentence at a minimum-security prison. He swore up and down on a stack of Bibles that he'd only been involved in two of the break-ins before he'd quit. His nervous stomach hadn't allowed him to continue.

"I kept thinking about those poor people being robbed," he babbled.

Yeah, right, Hawk thought. "Details," he pressed quietly, lowering his face against Phil's. "We need details."

Sherman moved his hands along the table. His sweaty palms left streaks as his eyes darted back and forth from one detective to the other. It was clear he was afraid of Hawk.

The young man's eyes darted back toward her as if he expected her to be his shield because she was the woman here. She hated stereotyping, but she used it to her advantage. "How did you get in?" she asked him.

"Danny's got a key-making machine in the trunk of his car," Phil blurted out. "We'd make impressions of the house keys, get the registration from the glove compartment and no one would be the wiser for it."

Hawk looked at Teri. "Until now." His attention focused on Phil. "What was your cut?"

"Just a little extra every week. I never broke into anyone's house, I swear." He raised his shaky hand in the air, as if he was taking an oath on an imaginary Bible.

Pacing the room, Hawk fired another question at him. "How'd you pick your victims?"

Phil craned his neck to try to keep his eyes on him. "Random at first. Then Danny told us to target the more expensive cars."

"How many keys and addresses did you give him?" Teri wanted to know.

Unsure, Phil shrugged nervously. "Maybe twenty. I told you, I didn't do this for that long."

"Twenty," she repeated. There was no reason to assume that the other men on the list hadn't given Tierney the same amount, if not more. She did the math. "But only thirty-six break-ins in all that time."

"That we know of," Hawk pointed out. "Maybe

some people didn't think the police would find their things, so they didn't bother reporting it.'' He came from a world where contact with the police was avoided at all costs, no matter what. He knew the way people in that world thought. Survival was more important than monetary goods. Knowing Tierney, there might have been another reason for the difference in numbers. ''And maybe he weeded them out, staking out the houses, seeing which made for an easier target.''

There was only one way they were going to find out. ''We need to get information from the horse's mouth,'' Teri told him.

Because for the moment they seemed to have forgotten about him, Sherman looked from one to the other, pathetically eager, pathetically nervous. ''Did I do okay?''

''You did fine,'' Hawk said without bothering to look in his direction. Stepping out in the hall, he waved in a uniformed policeman standing by. ''You can take him to booking now.''

Hawk was leaving the room, Teri realized a second after the other policeman came in for the prisoner. She was quick to fall in step with him. ''Where are you going?''

Hawk slid his arms through his jacket, then left it open. He didn't spare her a look. ''If the address we got is right, to see Tierney.''

She glanced toward her desk in the distance. ''Give me a second.''

"I'm going alone."

Second verse, same as the first. And she'd heard this song before. "No," she said quietly, forcefully, "you're not."

He'd never liked being on the receiving end of orders. Some were unavoidable. But hers weren't. And he didn't like what he thought he was hearing. "Don't trust me?"

Anger creased her forehead. "That's a stupid thing to say. Why wouldn't I trust you? Because you knew him?" They were a team. When was he going to get that through his thick head? "I'm your partner, I'm supposed to have your back. We're going together."

They'd only be wasting time, arguing. He blew out a breath. "There's no winning with you, is there?"

"Nope." She hurried quickly to her desk and grabbed her own jacket. "Get used to it," she told him, slipping the jacket on as she matched her stride with his.

Although, she knew damn well that if he wanted to go alone, he would have gone. Whether he knew it or not, he wanted her with him.

Getting out of the car, Hawk made his way into the twenty-story building. It was less than five years old. Danny Tierney had come up in the world. He now lived in an upscale apartment in the better part of the city. His situation was a far cry from the dirty mattress they had once shared in an abandoned warehouse.

Out of habit, his hand covered the bulge under his jacket.

Teri hurried alongside him as they went to the elevator. "You up to this?"

He scowled at her. What did this make—three? "Will you stop asking that?"

He wasn't an easy man to help, she thought darkly as she got into the empty elevator car. "I'm your partner. I'm concerned."

He pressed for the seventh floor. The doors shut immediately. The ride up was over in less than a minute. "Edmunds never asked me if I was feeling up to something. We just went in and did whatever needed doing."

She walked out in front of him. "Edmunds is a toad."

He looked up and down the carpeted hallway. It was empty. Hawk motioned her to the left. Tierney's apartment was the third one from the visible end. "I'll tell him that the next time I see him."

"Do that." Holding her weapon ready, poised, she nodded at Hawk.

He knocked on the door with his fist, banging a bit loudly. All he could think of was that here, but for the grace of a few good turns, went he. If anything, Danny had had the better foundation. At one point Danny at least had had a mother who'd loved him as best as she could. A mother who had married the wrong man. Danny's stepfather flexed his muscles and beat him whenever the opportunity arose, which, to hear Danny tell it, was frequently.

It was still no excuse for what had gone down.

"Danny, it's Hawk," Hawk said loudly. "Open up the door."

He was about to knock again when the sound of a chain being removed was heard on the other side of the door. A second later, the door opened.

The man on the other side was slightly shorter than Hawk, but no less powerfully built. His curly black hair made him look engaging, as did the wide grin on his face. He wore an expensive black silk robe that threatened to come undone from the loosely tied belt drooping at his waist.

The wide smile faded, but only a little, as he saw the gun being pointed at him. "Hey, man, what's going on? No need for guns." He looked at Teri. "Tell your honey to stop waving that thing around. Come in, talk, take a load off. I've got something going you might really be interested in."

Danny had changed, Hawk thought. He looked a hell of a lot better than he had the last time he'd seen him. Living off others could do that.

"Right. I would," Hawk agreed, not moving, "but not for the reasons you might think." He flashed his badge at the other man.

Staring at it, Tierney then started to laugh. "Nice bit of copying, Hawk. I always did say you were a natural."

"His badge is real," Teri said tersely, still pointing

her weapon at him. With her free hand, she dug out her own shield. "So's this one." She held it up in front of him.

The smile became tight around the edges. "What's this all about?"

"About ten to twenty," Hawk told him. "Somebody rolled on you, Danny."

There was bravado in his laugh. "Only one rolling is my girlfriend. She's still in bed." He nodded toward the inside of the apartment. "Have a taste. Your type, Hawk." His eyes momentarily washed over Teri before returning to Hawk's face. "Not like this one. C'mon, what do you say?"

Pity and loathing blazed in Hawk's blue eyes. "You don't get it, do you, Danny? We're taking you in."

The smiling face turned malevolent. "What's the charge?"

"Burglary. Murder. All sorts of things. You're under arrest. You have the right to remain silent—" she began to recite as Hawk turned him around and snapped handcuffs around his wrists.

Tierney looked at him in disbelief. "Hey, at least let me get my clothes."

"There's an orange jumpsuit waiting for you at the precinct," Hawk assured him grimly. "Just your size, too."

His words were met with a barrage of curses. This, Hawk thought, ushering him out of the apartment, was more like the Danny he knew.

* * *

"So, what is your type?"

Hawk stopped dead in his tracks. It had been a long day. He'd grilled the man who had once been his friend in darker times—to no avail. Tierney had used his one phone call to summon his lawyer, confident he'd walk out a free man at the end of the day.

He was still in his cell.

The case would be built. Solidly from everything that Hawk could see. They had enough on Tierney to put him away for a long time. Prodded further by Mulrooney, Phil Sherman had given them the address of the warehouse where the stolen goods were being stored until they could be properly fenced.

Ironically enough, it turned out to be the same warehouse he and Danny had once used for shelter. It was a small world and at times, it felt as if the fit was very, very tight.

Hawk looked now in her direction. The office was supposed to be empty. Only half the lights were on. "I thought everyone was gone."

"You thought wrong." Getting out her purse, she closed the bottom drawer with her foot and stood up. She threw the purse strap over her shoulder. "We broke the case. I thought you might want to get a drink and celebrate."

He thought of Danny. Each of them had crawled out of the life they'd found themselves in. But Danny's choice had taken him to an even darker side by some accounts. Hawk wondered if the man had ordered the execution of the two men they'd caught earlier.

Had Danny done it himself, or just ordered it done?

"I don't much feel like celebrating."

"Okay, then we'll get a drink and talk." She saw the look he gave her, the one that warned her to back off. She wasn't about to listen. "And don't tell me you don't feel like talking because you do."

He felt tired, drained and definitely not up to this. Hawk slid his jacket from the back of his chair. "Taken up mind reading?"

"Taken up partner reading," she told him. "Tierney looked as if he thought you and he were more than just passing acquaintances."

"Maybe we were," he allowed. "Once." And that was as much as she was getting out of him, he thought. She had a habit of taking everything and using it against him, undermining him.

Standing close to him, Teri looked up into his face. She didn't need lighting to see what was there. "You saw yourself in him today, didn't you? Saw what you could have become if you hadn't become a cop."

He didn't want to encourage her. The shrug was an accident, a slip.

"Well, I don't think you could have." The fierceness in her voice surprised him. "It's not in you to be dishonest."

He looked at her sharply. Where did she get off, acting as if she knew him inside and out? "You have no idea what's 'in' me, Cavanaugh, so don't pretend you know me.''

She wasn't about to allow him to sweep her aside. "But I do. You could have gone down the same path your parents did. Most kids of flawed parents wind up having the same flaws. You could have become like Jocko, but you didn't. And you could have gone Danny's route, but you didn't. That says a lot about your character.''

Character—now there was a nice, antiseptic description. It covered myriad conditions. "You have no idea what I did in the past.''

"No, I don't. So tell me." He said nothing. He was going to be stubborn about this, she thought in exasperation. "Okay, don't tell me, but tell someone. Tell a goldfish. Open up to something, Hawk. Don't let things eat at you. You're a good man and you do good every day. Accept that. Make peace with it. Stop blaming yourself because you couldn't save your parents.''

She'd struck a nerve he hadn't realized was exposed. His temper flared. "You don't know what you're talking about. That has nothing to do with it.''

"Okay." She folded her arms in front of her. "So tell me what does.''

He blew out a breath and sank down at his desk. Maybe she was right. Maybe talking to someone would help leech out this darkness inside of him, at least abate it a little.

"I met Danny when I ran away from the last foster home the system put me into," he began.

Teri sat down again and listened to him as he talked, keeping quiet even when she wanted to comment, to offer comfort. She knew he had to get this all out, and if she interrupted him in any way, he'd stop.

So she listened. And waited. Until she was certain he was finished. And when she was sure he was, she said, "I've only got one question."

"Only one?" Hawk laughed shortly, shaking off the somber blanket that had enshrouded him. "I'd thought you'd have a dozen. Okay," he said gamely, "what's your one question?"

She embellished the question she'd first asked him when he walked back into the squad room after personally taking Danny to booking. "Are wild-eyed Latin girls your type?"

At first he couldn't believe what he heard and then he laughed. Really laughed. It felt good.

Chapter Fourteen

"You're not answering," she pointed out a few moments later when he made no attempt to respond. She was smiling at him, but this nervous, uncertain fluttering went on in the pit of her stomach. And it was growing by the moment. "Are wild-eyed Latin girls your type?"

From across the length of two desks, Hawk studied her for a long moment. "Actually, no, they're not. Not anymore."

"Oh?" She told herself she was being stupid, taking heart from that. But she did. The nervous flutter heightened. "And do you have a type?"

Hawk paused, giving her question serious consideration. "Type" had never mattered to him. Looking back, he realized that the women he'd shared a night with had all been dark-haired.

Slowly, his eyes raised to her face. And he felt that strange, familiar tug. The one Cavanaugh could legitimately claim as her own. "I never thought about it before, but yes, I guess I do."

She could feel her pulse joining in the race. Damn, but the man excited her. Just by drawing breath. "And that is?"

Just the barest hint of a smile curved his mouth. "Blond. Medium height. Intelligent. Annoying." Each pronouncement emerged separately. He paused, looking at her significantly. "That sums it up."

She rose from her desk, aware that his eyes were moving along her body. Aware of the way her body was responding to him even at this distance. The man had powers.

"Does it?"

"Yeah, it does."

Teri rounded the desks, coming to stand beside his. Beside him.

"So, you want to have that drink now?" Hawk shook his head. "Dinner?" Again, he moved his head from side to side, his eyes never leaving her face.

She felt confused, and a whole lot of other things that had nothing remotely to do with logic. And all the while, anticipation built within her, making demands as it grew.

"Then what?"

Hawk rose slowly from his chair. He loomed over

her, fighting the temptation to take her here and now, in this room bathed in semidarkness.

"Come home with me," he said simply.

They were words he'd never thought he'd hear himself say, words he never thought he'd need to say and yet, there they were. He wanted her. Needed her. Despite all the pep talks he'd given himself, all the logic he'd tried to exercise over his reactions to her, only one thing prevailed. He needed her.

At least for tonight.

Because tonight he didn't want to be alone with his memories of the past. He had shut them away in a tight box a long time ago, but seeing Danny today had brought everything back to him, had shown him the road not taken, the road he might have taken if he hadn't been strong enough. And he didn't like what he saw. Didn't like the fact that only a trick of fate had kept him from ending up that way.

"Okay," she said slowly, watching his face for signs of regret. She took her cue from him, tried not to think about what she was feeling herself. She couldn't tackle something so complicated right now.

There was no moon tonight, she noticed as she followed behind Hawk's car in her own. It added to the feeling of desolation. Was that why he'd asked her to come? Because he felt lonely?

It should have mattered to her, but it didn't. She didn't care why he'd asked, only that he had.

She made one pass through his complex, then

headed out into the street again, looking for parking. She found a space on the block that ran along right outside. This hour of the night, all visitor parking within the apartment complex was taken.

As she walked along the mist-dampened path to his third-floor, single room, she could hear her heels clicking as they struck the pavement. Could hear her heart echoing the beat in her ears.

If she had an ounce of sense in her head, Teri told herself, she would turn around right now, get into her car and drive home. Home, where things were safe. Home, where she wasn't required to risk her heart.

She kept walking.

Hawk was in the doorway, waiting for her. If she hadn't known better, she would have said he looked anxious.

She would have been right. He was. As soon as he'd parked his own car, he'd stood there waiting, wondering. "I thought maybe you changed your mind."

I did. Three times. "Parking's hard to come by," she murmured, and then she looked up at him. "Why, did you want me to change my mind?"

A funny smile she couldn't quite place played along his lips. "It would make things easier."

"What things?" she asked.

He didn't answer her, couldn't answer her, because he hadn't allowed himself to label what he was feeling. Not for her. And he certainly wasn't about to label the nameless apprehension that lurked inside of him, growing bigger by the moment.

All he knew was that he didn't want to get attached.

What he wanted didn't seem to matter, not in the face of the desires pulsing inside of him.

The moment Teri walked into the apartment, he swept her into his arms without warning, pushing the door closed strictly as an afterthought. Hunger, fueled by emotions he'd struggled to keep chained, had grown to giant, unmanageable proportions.

He didn't know how much longer he could rein himself in.

As he pressed hot, ardent kisses along her neck, making her head spin, Teri struggled to keep a cool head. She couldn't let him know how much she wanted this, how much she wanted him. How she'd been able to think of almost nothing else except being with him like this again.

If Hawk knew, if he suspected, that would give him all the cards, leaving her with nothing. She'd have to rely on him for everything, every morsel, every crumb. And if he walked away, she would cave.

That couldn't happen.

"What things?" she breathed, asking again.

"Damned if I know," he rasped, his breath curling along her heated skin.

Clothing was eliminated with breathtaking speed as eagerness took charge of the reins and plotted the course for them.

She hadn't realized just how much she'd ached to have him touch her, caress her again until just now. Her whole body felt as if it vibrated, desperate for release, yet desperate for the sensations that led to the climax, as well.

Though the distance wasn't far, they barely made it to the bed. He wanted to take her where she stood, to sheath himself inside of her and grab on to the comfort of that joining with both hands, pretending for a moment that was all he needed. That the world was a good place as long as he could be in it with her.

He knew he was attaching a great deal of importance to this and he shouldn't be. He knew how quickly things could fall apart, how quickly they could be blown apart.

But knowing changed nothing. Something inside of him needed this thing he'd denied himself for so long. Beacons stood alone. Were alone. He didn't want to be alone anymore.

His mouth flew all along her body, drugging her, making it hard for her to think clearly. This wasn't like Hawk at all. The last time he'd assaulted her senses, but there hadn't been this rush, this fire that threatened to consume them both.

She tried to get him to slow down, but even as she braced her hands on his shoulders, even as the words rose to her lips, they melted away. His mouth did things to her that erased everything else in its path. Certainly logic.

His tongue took possession of her. The explosion that wracked her body was not long in coming. She arched into it, into him, then fell back on the tangled covers, exhausted. Only to have him begin again.

Everything inside of her went wild.

The next explosions came faster. Small, large, they converged inside her body until she thought she couldn't take the ecstasy any longer, not without completely expiring.

She wanted more, always more.

And then he was over her, taking her. She wrapped her legs around his torso, arching so that he could drive himself deep into her. She resisted the urge to bite down on his shoulder as he took the last shred that comprised the essence of her and left her all but numb. And very, very contented.

She didn't think that her heart would ever stop pounding.

"What was all that about?" she asked when she finally summoned the strength to form words without gasping for air.

He lay over her, hardly aware of his surroundings beyond the way her breasts rose and fell, brushing against him as she breathed. He didn't remember ever feeling happy before. Was that what this was? he wondered. Happiness? He had no frame of reference to draw on.

"Hmm?" Hawk raised his head, surprised at how much effort the simple action required. "Did I do it wrong?'' Resting an elbow on the bed, he propped his head up and looked at her.

''I know what you did.'' She laughed. ''You just seemed a little more—'' Teri hunted for a word ''—inspired this time.''

''Maybe you inspire me.'' Things were going on inside of him again, things he would need to examine eventually, but not yet. Not yet. Taking a strand of her hair, he wrapped it around his index finger slowly. ''Why do you have this need to turn everything into an interrogation?''

She struggled not to wiggle beneath him as her body reacted to the pressure of his. ''I'm not interrogating, I'm trying to understand.''

''Well, don't.'' It was friendly advice, but with a warning. ''Some things don't hold up well under scrutiny.''

''What does that mean?''

He smiled into her eyes then. He found himself wanting her again. Damn, but she could raise the dead. ''It means that I'm going to have to kiss you again to shut you up.''

This time she did move beneath him. And felt his desire for her growing. ''Is that the only reason you're going to kiss me again?''

He shifted slightly, tantalizing her with each movement. ''I plead the Fifth.''

She didn't want to know things anymore. She just wanted to be with him. ''You don't have to plead at all.''

But he did. He had to plead for mercy, at least in his mind, because he was completely at hers and that was a source of great concern to him. But not now. Now, he just wanted to lose himself in her again. To take slowly what he'd snatched up so quickly before. To savor it this time because tonight was all there was.

Now was all there was.

It was the one lesson in life he'd learned, the only true lesson that life had to offer. He'd learned it the hard way. Nothing lasted. Ever. And it was best to move on rather than allow yourself to be run over, to allow yourself to be devastated.

But all that was for dawn's early light. The night was made for passion and he had it to spare.

He had no choice.

She gave him no choice.

He had to switch partners before it was too late for him.

If it wasn't already.

He could feel his resolve slackening, could feel himself slipping quickly. He couldn't afford to let that happen, couldn't let himself become weak.

Besides, he had nothing to offer her. She was light; he was the complete absence of it. She came from a large, happy, well-adjusted family. His had been the last word in dysfunctional. They didn't belong together and the fact that he wanted them to be together only brought home to him the fact that he needed to get out now, before he couldn't anymore.

Sitting in front of the steel-gray desk, he watched the chief of detectives' face as the man reviewed the paperwork on the desk in front of him. He couldn't help thinking that Brian Cavanaugh was the spitting image of his older brother, Andrew.

Finally, the man looked up at him. The expression on his face was incredulous. "You're asking for another partner?"

Ordinarily, the situation was reversed and it was his partners, for one reason or another, who were asking to bail out. But this was different.

"Yes, sir." It was either that, or transfer out of the department entirely.

Maybe going back to Homicide was the answer. Hawk debated the possibility.

Brian Cavanaugh set down the lengthy form he was looking over. "Would you mind if I asked why?"

Hawk wasn't about to get into it and he didn't like lying. That gave him no options. "It would just be better all around."

It was obvious by his expression that the chief of detectives had his own opinion on the matter. "You know, I put you together with Teri for a reason. Not because she's my niece," he said firmly, forestalling any debate in that direction, "but because I had a feeling that she could make a difference for you."

Hawk drew his eyebrows together. "Excuse me?"

The chief's manner was calm, soothing. He'd been

known to quell more than one tempest in his time, but Hawk didn't feel like being analyzed. He bit his tongue, waiting.

"You're a damn good detective, Hawk, and I'm happy to have you as part of my team, but I see a great deal of potential in you that isn't being tapped." Hawk struggled not to shift impatiently in his chair. "A man keeps things bottled up inside of him for years, there's no telling when he might go off."

"I'm not planning to detonate, sir," Hawk answered as politely as he could under the circumstances. "At least, not if I can change partners."

Brian looked down on the page again. Hawk had cited irreconcilable differences as the reason for the request. He began to place the page in his desk drawer. "Tell you what—why don't you sleep on it?"

The look in Hawk's eyes stopped him from closing the drawer. "I don't have to sleep on it, sir. I've already made up my mind."

Resigned, Brian reluctantly nodded. "All right. But I think this is a mistake. Teri's the first partner you've had who didn't come in to me to complain about you." He waited, but there was nothing. "But if this is what you want—"

"I do."

Brian checked the roster. "I'm switching you with Toby Mitchell, effective immediately. You'll be teamed up with Alan Williams. I'll send through the paperwork right away." He made a notation on the form, then looked up at Hawk. "Do you want to tell her, or shall I?"

Hawk shrugged. "Either way." Although he would have preferred not to have to face her. Luck was riding with him. He got his wish.

"I'll handle it," Brian said. His tone was far from pleased.

Hawk didn't have to open his door.

He knew he would find Teri on the other side the moment he heard the pounding. What he hadn't expected was to find her all but breathing fire. He'd never seen her this angry. This magnificent. Sparks almost flew from her eyes.

The second he opened the door, she pushed her way in, then whirled on her heel to look up at him.

"There are a lot of words I would have used to describe you, Hawk, most of them not very pretty, but the one word I was completely certain didn't apply to you was *coward*." Her chin was up, her tolerance down. She couldn't remember ever being more furious, ever feeling more betrayed in her life. "Why weren't you man enough to tell me you were putting in for another partner? I thought we had an understanding, that we'd reached a rhythm. If there was something wrong, why didn't you just tell me?"

"Because it wasn't something to talk about, it was just something to do," he ground out. "Besides, this was the way it always happened for me. One minute I had one partner, the next I had another." And it had all been the same to him, marginally tolerable. Until now.

"Well, that's not the way it's ever happened to me," she declared hotly. "The only other partners I had retired. Besides," she said, poking at his chest with her index finger, "what happened in the past doesn't count here." She reinforced each word with a jab to his chest. Each jab was harder than the last, shadowing her fury.

He let her get through the sentence, then grabbed her hand and pushed it away. "You're making a hole in my chest."

"Good. It'll match the one in your head." But she let her hand remain at her side. "I thought we were more than just two people riding around in a car together."

Had she just been fooling herself? Was this what he was like with women? Made love to them until they were mindless, then bailed out? No, if that were true, she would have heard. Even though he was so closemouthed, in-house gossip would have brought word to her long before anything had exploded between them.

He was turning away from her. Incensed, she grabbed his shoulder and yanked him around.

"Damn it, Hawk, you owed me a little courtesy. You should have come to me to work out whatever problem is bothering you."

"You *are* the problem that needs to be worked out."

She felt as if all the air had been let out of her lungs. "What?"

He struggled to keep his temper in check, his voice even. Struggled to keep from telling her more than he wanted her to know. But it wasn't easy.

"You've gotten under my skin. Gotten to me and I don't want to be gotten to. So just go home, Teri. Go home to your nice house, your nice family and leave me the hell alone."

She wanted to fight him on this, to tell him that he wasn't making any sense. That maybe he was feeling as scared as she was about the path they were on, but that it was okay because she'd hold his hand and he would hold hers and somehow they'd get through it together.

He'd called her by her first name again. That had to mean something. She was grasping at straws, she told herself. If she had to do this much persuading, maybe they wouldn't get through it together.

Or maybe most of it was in her head, maybe most of the feelings were all one-sided. Her side, not his.

Even she knew that there came a time when pushing wasn't the way to go. Although it was against every single natural impulse she harbored, Teri stepped back, raised her hands and surrendered.

"Okay," she said quietly. "Okay. You win. Do whatever you want."

With that, she turned on her heel and walked out of his apartment. Before he could see her cry.

Hawk stood where he was for a long moment, staring at the door she'd just closed. And then, letting loose with an oath, he doubled up his fist and slammed it into the wall.

Chapter Fifteen

Hawk walked into his apartment, closing the door behind him. He removed his weapon and holster, placing it carefully beside the keys he'd dropped on the small counter. Dinner received a passing thought from him, then was abandoned in favor of something more liquid.

Taking the bottle of beer out of the refrigerator, he dropped onto the love seat and aimed the remote at the television set. He had no preferences as to a program, only that there be a droning voice in the background. Silence just wasn't cutting it for him anymore.

He opened the bottle and took a deep drag from it, then stared down at the amber glass. He was rid of her, at least in theory. He and Williams had been partnered for two weeks now and were already working as if they'd been together from the very beginning.

He had what he wanted. Trouble was, he didn't want it anymore.

Hawk took another long pull on the bottle. A bright, smiling woman on the set was pushing tooth whitener. Her smile reminded him of Teri.

Everything reminded him of Teri.

He'd thought that, given the right opportunity, he could easily reclaim his old habits, his old ways.

He thought wrong. It was like a snake trying to get back into the skin he'd shed. Impossible. Like it or not, he'd moved on in his life. Maybe even grown. That was something she would have probably said, he thought.

All he knew was that his old life didn't fit him anymore. Working and coming home wasn't enough, the way it had once been. Sharing a partnership with Williams wasn't enough.

The man was everything his old partner at Homicide had been. Quiet, reflective and a pretty decent enough detective when the chips were down. God knows Williams didn't talk his ear off, the way she had. At times, it seemed as if he and Williams were even on the same wavelength.

But there was no spark, no fire. No sheen. Everything seemed dull somehow. It was as if he'd been led out into the sunshine only to be pushed back into his cave again. The cave wasn't good enough any-more. He wanted his sunshine back.

Except that meant admitting he was wrong.

Hawk frowned to himself. He wasn't very prone to admitting he was wrong, he thought. So he'd contin-ued to try. And continued to feel as if he were stum-bling around in the dark, searching for the one way out of that cave.

Sitting back on the love seat, he put his feet up on the coffee table, crossing his boots at the ankle and staring at the set.

He still saw her.

They inhabited the same squad room, albeit at dif-ferent ends. It was easy enough to avoid looking her way if he put his mind to it, but avoiding hearing her was another matter. He couldn't do that without put-ting in earplugs. He'd lost the knack of tuning things out. Tuning her out. He caught himself actually lis-tening for her. For the sound of her laughter, which was the worst because it got under his skin. Reminded him of things he didn't want to be reminded of. Like being with her. Like making love with her. Like being tied up in knots and welcoming the sensation.

It was all wrong.

He'd thought of going back to the chief and asking him for a transfer back into his old Homicide division, had even gone up to the man's office once. But some-thing at the last minute had kept him from going in.

Maybe it was the fear that the chief would think of him as a royal pain. He'd never needed special treatment before. But that had been before that damned witch had cast her spell over him.

It was all Cavanaugh's fault, he thought miserably. All of it. He'd been happy before she came.

No, he hadn't, Hawk admitted as he drained the last of his bottle. Setting it down, he debated having another. But an entire sea of beer wasn't going to cure what ailed him and nothing but a cure was acceptable right now.

He hadn't been happy at all before Teri had stormed her way into his life. That was the whole problem. Being with her had shown him a glimpse of what being happy could be like.

She'd make him laugh. More than that, she'd made him feel.

And fear of feeling was what had gotten him to this juncture in his life.

He didn't want to be in it anymore.

Muting the TV, he took out his cell phone and punched in a number.

Maybe she should have taken her father up on the invitation and gone to the movie. It was one of those action-buddy movies he favored. She did, too. But she didn't feel as if she'd be good company tonight. Besides, her uncle was coming and the last thing she wanted to hear was to have him ask how the new partner was working out.

He wasn't. Oh, he was likable enough and, unlike Hawk, Mitchell talked. Talked a great deal and actually seemed interested in what she had to say. But that was just the problem. He was unlike Hawk and all Mitchell did was make her miss Hawk more.

She had to get over this, she told herself sternly, had to get over being like some stupid, mooning adolescent who'd just broken up with the captain of the football team. She was a grown woman and these things happened. It was all part of life.

A life without Hawk.

"Okay, enough is enough. This has gone on for two weeks. You've got twelve hours to shape up, Cavanaugh, you hear me?" she demanded of her reflection in the hall mirror.

The reflection didn't look too convinced that it could be done.

She heard the doorbell and didn't bother stifling the groan. It wasn't one of her siblings, because they all had keys and never bothered to ring. Her father believed in the open-door policy. If it was one of her cousins, she just wasn't in the mood to make small talk. But there was no use trying to hide because her car was parked outside in the driveway. They'd know she was home.

Maybe this was better, she told herself. If she had to pretend for someone, she wouldn't have time to dwell on how rotten she felt.

The doorbell rang again, more insistently this time. "I'm coming, I'm coming," she called out, hurrying to the door.

He was the last person in the world she'd expected to see on her doorstep.

It was like a fantasy she might have conjured up, but even as she conjured, she would have known in her heart that it couldn't possibly happen.

Except that it had.

She wondered if somewhere there was a gaggle of devils purchasing ice picks.

"Hi."

"Hi," he responded.

Well, she thought, at least he hadn't lost his knack for scintillating conversation. After a beat, she stepped back and gestured inside the house. "Do you want to come in?"

"Yeah."

She waited. Hawk remained standing where he was, as if he were glued in place. "Might help if you moved your feet."

Like someone coming out of a trance, Hawk came to and crossed the threshold into her house. There was no turning back now, he thought. His hands felt cold. He shoved them into his pockets and glanced around the area. "Your family around?"

She shut the door and turned around to look at him. "Rayne's over at Cole's place. My father went to the movies with my uncle." Nameless suspicions began to form. "Why?"

"No reason." They were alone, he thought. That was good. He'd have better luck getting this out if they were alone.

She noticed that he was only wearing his jacket. It was a cold night. What was he doing here?

Teri led the way into the living room. "Do you want anything to drink?"

For the first time since he'd left childhood, he felt as if his courage was flagging. He would have liked a drink. A stiff one. But he wasn't about to fall back on artificial props now, not after he'd come so far in his life. That was for losers like his parents had been. "No thanks, I'm okay."

She felt awkward around him. As if she'd somehow slipped her skin on backward and it wasn't fitting quite right. She didn't like the sensation.

He was here to say something, she thought. But what? That he was leaving the city? No, it couldn't be that. Hawk wouldn't come to tell her; he'd just leave. Vanish like smoke. That was more his style.

God, but she'd missed him. Missed him so much that her stomach ached. These past two weeks had been the hardest she'd gone through in a very long time. The feeling wasn't unlike having some kind of death in the family. And in a way, she supposed there had. A death to what she'd hoped was to be.

"Would you like to sit?" She indicated the sofa behind him.

He looked over his shoulder, then shook his head. "No, I'll stand."

She licked her lips, searching for something to say. "So how's it going?"

He thought of putting up a pretense. But that wasn't

why he was here. "Not good. Bad." He looked at her. "Hell, actually."

That was surprisingly honest of him, she thought. Teri made the only guess she could. "Williams talk too much?"

He wanted to touch her. To run his fingers through her hair, to bury his face in her neck and smell that soft scent of soap that clung to her skin.

Fighting urges, he shoved his hands into his pockets. "He doesn't talk at all."

She laughed shortly. "Should be heaven for you, not the other place you mentioned."

She was sharp. Didn't she get it? Was he going to have to stand here and spill out his guts to her? Taking his hand out, he ran it through his hair. "Yeah, well, it's not."

She saw the quick flash of healing bruises. This was new. She stifled the temptation of taking the hand in hers and examining it. "What's with your knuckles? Or am I not allowed to ask that?"

"Nothing." She kept on looking at him, drawing the words to the surface as if she were levitating them from inside of him. "I slammed my fist into a wall."

"Why?" she deadpanned. "Did the wall do something to annoy you?"

"No," Hawk snapped, irritated. "I did something to annoy me."

She studied his face. He looked worn, tired. She squelched the protective feelings. That wasn't what

Hawk wanted from her. What *did* he want from her? ''Doesn't seem very fair to take it out on the wall.''

''No, it doesn't. And it's not fair to take my problem out on you.''

She frowned. This was getting more obscure instead of clear. ''Now you lost me. I was doing fine talking about walls, but this is kind of dicey. This is about people—''

She was making fun of him, he thought. And he deserved it. Knowing still didn't contain the anxiety that telegraphed itself through him. ''Will you shut up for a second and let me get this out?''

''Well, since you put it so nicely, how could I refuse?''

He took a deep breath, a runner preparing to make a dash for the finish line. ''I was wrong.''

She was glad there were no breezes floating through the house or she would have been picking herself up from the floor.

''Go on,'' she urged slowly. ''Not that I don't agree with that, blanketly, but I would like a few more specifics to go on.''

''I was wrong when I thought that if we weren't always in each other's faces, things would get better.''

What was he up to? It couldn't be as simple as what she was thinking. ''They haven't?''

''They haven't.''

Feeling as if she had nothing to lose, she pressed. ''What kind of things?''

Patience snapped and so did he as he repeated loudly, "Things."

Nice to know some things remained constant, she thought. "Contrary to popular belief, if you raise your voice to say something, that doesn't explain anything or make it clearer." She crossed her arms before her. "Try again. What things?"

He was a man who didn't believe in laundry lists, so he summed it up. "My life."

"You were looking to improve your life by getting rid of me." She said the words slowly, as if she were trying to digest them, or at least make some kind of sense out of them.

"No, damn it, I was just trying to get my life back to where it was."

"And you didn't?"

"No, I did," he contradicted, and then laid all his cards on that table. Or thought he did. "Except that I don't like it the way it was anymore."

"Hard man to please."

She shrugged and he thought that maybe he'd blown it. Maybe she didn't give a damn what he felt or did. But instead of walking away from the table and his losses, the way he always had, he decided to dig in and fight.

"I know. But you did."

Teri blinked and wondered when her hearing had gone out on her. "Did what?"

"Pleased me."

He had a way with words, she thought. "My union

rep at Feminists Daily will be very happy to hear that.''

He stared at her for a second, then shook his head as if that could somehow help clear away the cobwebs that had descended over it. This wasn't coming out the way he'd wanted. But then, everything around Teri was unpredictable. That was part of the attraction. ''Damn it, you know what I mean.''

''Maybe.'' She was beginning to, or at least thought she was. But she'd gone down the wrong path before. This time, she wanted the bread crumbs to clearly lead the way to markers, not more bread crumbs. ''But I want to hear you elaborate it. Articulate for once in your life with something less than a bearlike growl, Hawk. Talk to me. Tell me what you're thinking.''

He tried again. ''I'm thinking that life with you was bad—''

She shook her head, managing to keep the smile back. ''Not your best start.''

He pushed on with determination. ''But life without you is hell.''

''Better.'' She waited. Nothing followed. This was going to be a long process, she thought. ''That wasn't the end of it, was it?''

''No,'' he snapped, then fell into silence again as he tried to phrase things in his head, phrase them the way he knew she wanted to hear them.

She cocked her head and looked at him, amusement

entering her eyes. "These other words, are they coming anytime soon?"

"I want you back." It was a blunt statement, but it summed up everything.

"How, Hawk?" She searched his face, trying to delve into his soul, warning herself not to get too carried away. "How do you want me back? As a partner?"

It was a start, he thought with relief, one he could build on. "Yes."

She pretended to consider his request and then shook her head. "Might be difficult—Mitchell and I get along beautifully."

She was kidding, he realized. And maybe, just maybe, the window of opportunity hadn't shut down. "I could kill him," he offered mildly.

Teri nodded her head slowly. "Yes, that would dissolve the partnership. But it might make it hard being your partner if you're in prison." She allowed herself a broad smile. "It'll be simpler if we just get the chief to switch us back."

Damn, it *was* going to be all right, he thought. He knew her well enough for that, to know when he was in the hot seat and when he wasn't. "Okay, we'll do it your way."

The smile went from ear to ear. "That has a nice ring to it."

"Since you brought it up—" He began to feel around inside his pocket, hoping what he'd brought with him hadn't fallen out somewhere. And then he breathed a sigh of relief as his fingers came in contact with the metal.

"Brought what up?"

And then the banter died on her lips as she stared at what he held in the palm of his hand. It was a ring. A perfect, beautiful, heart-shaped diamond ring.

Words stuck to the roof of her mouth and had to be pried out one by one. "I don't suppose you got that from the bottom of a Cracker Jack box."

"No."

She held her breath as he took her hand and slipped the ring on her finger.

Her heart hammered as she stared down at the gem. "Look at that. It fits," she whispered in awe.

He hadn't left that to chance. "I asked your sister if she knew your ring size."

Teri's head jerked up. She couldn't have been more surprised than if he'd just ripped off his shirt to announce that he was really Tarzan. "You asked my sister?"

"Callie."

She stared at him as if he'd suddenly turned into an alien life form. Or the man of her secret dreams. "You actually communicated something personal to a member of my family?" To cover just how deeply moved she was, she placed her hand over her chest, feigning shock. "My God, Hawk, there's hope for you yet."

"Only if you marry me."

Her knees suddenly went out on her. Afraid of

246 THE STRONG SILENT TYPE

sinking to the floor, she grabbed his arm. "I think I need to sit down."

But he wouldn't let her sit. Instead, he swept her into his arms, holding her close to him. "I won't let you fall." She looked up at him, her eyes dazed with disbelief. He could hardly believe any of this himself. But he felt freer than he ever had in his life. And happier. "I've never, ever felt about anyone the way I feel about you. These past couple of weeks have been hell."

Happiness curled through her, filling every nook and cranny. "You mentioned that."

How had he managed to survive these past two weeks without her? Without holding her like this? "Did I also mention that I love you?"

"No," she allowed. "That's new, although the ring did give me a hint."

"Marry me, Teri—"

Butterflies turned into eagles. Eagles with grins on their beaks. "There you go again, using my first name and getting me all misty." She looked up at him, her tone becoming serious. She was a goner and she knew it. "You don't play fair, you know."

He combed his hand through her hair, cupping her cheek. "I'll play any way you want me to, Teri, as long as you say yes."

"To the partnership?" she teased.

"To everything."

She cocked her head again. "Now, that might be

tricky. My father always taught me not to issue blanket statements I might regret.''

''You won't regret this, Teri. I swear you won't regret this.''

''I know.'' She threaded her arms around his neck, standing on her toes to do so. ''I'm so in love with you right now, I'm going to burst. So yes, the answer's yes. Yes, I'll become your partner again, and yes, I'll marry you.''

He framed her face with his hands. ''That's all I want to hear out of you for a while.''

''No problem,'' she whispered just before he brought his mouth down to hers and sealed both their fates.

Epilogue

Andrew struggled against the wall of loneliness that threatened to close around him.

Last night had been a surprise. He'd come home from the movies with Brian only to have Teri tell him that she was getting married. To Hawk.

Of course, in a way, he'd seen it coming. Seen the way the young man had looked at his daughter. Probably the way he'd looked at Rose once.

That made four now. Four out of five of his children were getting married, not to mention his nephew, Patrick. Out of the blue, just like that. He thought of how empty the house was going to seem soon. It made him miss Rose all the more.

Maybe he should go back up there, he thought.

He'd hoped that she'd call him, but she hadn't. She'd had time to think things over.

Maybe if he went, tried to persuade her a little, that might do the trick....

He stopped and cocked his head. Was that the door-bell?

Telling himself he was probably hearing things, he shut off the tap water and stopped rinsing the dishes before stacking them in the dishwasher.

The soft peal of the doorbell disturbed the atmosphere. Well, at least he knew his hearing was as good as ever, he congratulated himself. He grabbed a towel and dried his hands as he made his way to the front door.

They didn't see too many door-to-door salespeople in this part of the city and it was way too early for one of the neighborhood kids to be trying to sell cookies, or wrapping paper, or whatever their schools were pushing these days to raise funds, he thought.

Like as not, it was either Rayne or Teri. Both had gone out together just a few minutes ago. One of them had probably forgotten her keys. It wouldn't be the first time.

Slinging the towel over his right shoulder, Andrew reached for the doorknob and swung the door open. "What did you forget?"

The words hung in the air, mocking him, as he looked into the face of the woman who called herself Claire.

She looked nervous, vulnerable and completely uncertain. It took her a moment before she responded. "Everything, apparently."

* * * * *

*If you liked THE STRONG SILENT TYPE,
you'll love Marie Ferrarella's next
CAVANAUGH JUSTICE romance,
CAVANAUGH'S WOMAN,
coming to you from
Silhouette Special Edition
in June 2004.
Don't miss it!*

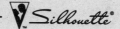

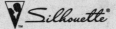

SPECIAL EDITION™

A captivating new book by author

Lynda Sandoval

ONE PERFECT MAN
(Silhouette Special Edition #1620)

After fourteen years of avoiding even
the remote possibility of entanglements
that might put his daughter in a vulnerable
position, Tomás Garza willingly brought
beautiful Erica Gonçalves into his house,
into all their lives, even if only for business
reasons. She was here, and the memory
of her, he knew, would linger even
when she'd left.

What had he been thinking?

Available June 2004
at your favorite retail outlet.

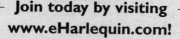

If you enjoyed what you just read,
then we've got an offer you can't resist!

Take 2 bestselling love stories FREE!

Plus get a FREE surprise gift!

Clip this page and mail it to Silhouette Reader Service™

IN U.S.A.
3010 Walden Ave.
P.O. Box 1867
Buffalo, N.Y. 14240-1867

IN CANADA
P.O. Box 609
Fort Erie, Ontario
L2A 5X3

YES! Please send me 2 free Silhouette Special Edition® novels and my free surprise gift. After receiving them, if I don't wish to receive anymore, I can return the shipping statement marked cancel. If I don't cancel, I will receive 6 brand-new novels every month, before they're available in stores! In the U.S.A., bill me at the bargain price of $3.99 plus 25¢ shipping and handling per book and applicable sales tax, if any*. In Canada, bill me at the bargain price of $4.74 plus 25¢ shipping and handling per book and applicable taxes**. That's the complete price and a savings of at least 10% off the cover prices—what a great deal! I understand that accepting the 2 free books and gift places me under no obligation ever to buy any books. I can always return a shipment and cancel at any time. Even if I never buy another book from Silhouette, the 2 free books and gift are mine to keep forever.

235 SDN DNUR
335 SDN DNUS

Name	(PLEASE PRINT)
Address	Apt.#
City	State/Prov.	Zip/Postal Code

* Terms and prices subject to change without notice. Sales tax applicable in N.Y.
** Canadian residents will be charged applicable provincial taxes and GST.
  All orders subject to approval. Offer limited to one per household and not valid to current Silhouette Special Edition® subscribers.
  ® are registered trademarks of Harlequin Books S.A., used under license.

SPED02   ©1998 Harlequin Enterprises Limited

COMING NEXT MONTH

Silhouette®

SPECIAL EDITION®

#1615 FIFTY WAYS TO SAY I'M PREGNANT—Christine Rimmer
Bravo Family Ties
Reunited after six long years, Starr Bravo and Beau Tisdale couldn't deny the attraction that had always sizzled between them. But when Starr discovered she was carrying Beau's baby, she panicked and fled the scene. Could Beau find—and forgive—his one true love so they could be a family at last?

#1616 ACCIDENTAL FAMILY—Joan Elliott Pickart
The Baby Bet: MacAllister's Gifts
When Patty Sharpe Clark set out to track down a child's missing father, David Montgomery, she was shocked to learn he'd been in an accident and had amnesia! She vowed to care for Sarah Ann until the girl's father recovered, but would Patty find love where she least expected?

#1617 CAVANAUGH'S WOMAN—Marie Ferrarella
Cavanaugh Justice
Deeply dedicated to his family and work, Shaw Cavanaugh didn't have time for the frivolity of life…until he met Moira McCormick. The charming actress came from a troubled past and longed to be part of a family, but would Shaw accept her into his life…forever?

#1618 HOT AUGUST NIGHTS—Christine Flynn
The Kendricks of Camelot
After CEO Matt Callaway and Ashley Kendrick shared a steamy one-night stand, the fear of scandal had separated them. Ashley had never forgotten the way Matt made her feel, but would he be able to forgive her for keeping their unborn child a secret…?

#1619 THE DADDY SURVEY—Janis Reams Hudson
Men of Cherokee Rose
Rancher Sloan Chisolm had never turned his back on a woman in trouble. So when beautiful Emily Nelson lost her job as a waitress, he was determined that she come work for him at the Cherokee Rose Ranch. He knew she considered being his housekeeper temporary, but their kisses made him hope that this might be a partnership…for life.

#1620 ONE PERFECT MAN—Lynda Sandoval
Years ago Tomas Garza's dreams of a family had fallen apart after his wife abandoned him and their daughter. He'd desperately tried to fill the void in his daughter's life, but the time had come when she needed a woman—someone like the beautiful event planner Erica Goncalves. She'd agreed to help him plan a party for his daughter, but would she be open to something more permanent?

SSECNM0504